HEIR OF THE THUNDERBIRD

Martin and May-Britt Brændstrup

Harvard Square Editions
New York
2018

Heir of the Thunderbird
by Martin and May-Britt Brændstrup

Copyright © 2018

Cover design by J. Caleb Clark ©

ISBN 978-1-941861-55-4
Printed in the United States of America

Published in the United States by
Harvard Square Editions
www.harvardsquareeditions.org

The Beginning

HEAVY RAIN FORCED even the toughest joggers inside and left the streets of Copenhagen deserted. The man's light-colored jacket stood in stark contrast to his dark skin and slick, black hair. To both friends and enemies, he was known as The Wolf.

He stubbed his cigarette against the street light and pulled a sheet of paper from his inside coat pocket. The rain made the ink run, but it didn't matter. He had read it a million times on the ferry as he crossed the sea from Germany.

25.4.2017

From: Albert Jensen (Alb_J@gmail.com)
To: Grandmaster Würher (wurher@telemail.de)
Subject: Re my observations in the ward

As agreed, I am keeping a close eye on all patients in the ward, and one in particular has caught my attention. It is a girl, but she is of Indian origin! She has undergone an extensive series of treatments, all of which have proven unsuccessful. Much would indicate that she is the one we have been looking for!

His grey wolf-like eyes glinted, as he gazed up at the hospital building. The dimly lit windows appeared bright against the crying sky. Like squares on a chessboard.

A door slid open. A man in a white lab coat stuck his head out and waved.

The Wolf turned his collar up against the rain, and started toward the open door.

"These are the young squaw's records." The man in the lab coat handed him a thick file. He blinked nervously behind his glasses while The Wolf flipped through the papers.

"As you can see, she's been here countless times with all sorts of bone injuries. The doctors have done loads of tests and examined her from head to toe, but they haven't been able to diagnose it. Are you sure you want her? You said to look out for a boy!"

"Albert, listen closely," The Wolf said. "We ARE looking for a boy, but the other signs are there so we have to check up on her. Boy or girl, we haven't been this close in years. You must convince the doctors that it's essential that the girl is sent to our clinic in Dresden." He held out an envelope. "And if she turns out to be the one, you will be even more amply rewarded!"

Albert flashed a greedy smile, but froze when he saw the slender knife in The Wolf's other hand.

The Wolf's eyes narrowed. "If you fail, there will be consequences...."

Albert nodded cautiously as he angled himself away from the knife. The Wolf thrust the envelope hard against Albert's chest. Then, he disappeared through the door and back into the rain.

Albert shuddered and pulled his lab coat tighter around him. There was no reason to threaten him. It wasn't the first time he had carried out services for the chapter, and they always paid him well. If they wanted the girl, he knew just who to talk to. A doctor who wouldn't hesitate to send such a hopeless patient to the 'specialists' if the price was right.

Anyway, it was easy money!

Chapter 1
The Girl Made of Glass

Ullerslev, 4 May 2017

Dear Diary,

I got my birthday presents this morning, and you were one of them! I love how you are bound in beautifully embossed leather and that your small lock will keep all my secrets safe. You even have a small holder on your right side for my new pen.

A very expensive ballpoint pen and a leather-bound diary. Not what you would normally buy for a teenager, but I was ecstatic. The blank pages and the scent of new leather. I was just itching to start writing then and there, but I had to be sociable for a couple of hours at least☺☺☺.

By the way, my mom told me that I have another present coming, but it won't arrive till later because she ordered it on the web yesterday.

For some time, I toyed with the idea of throwing a birthday party to celebrate turning 16.

Sweet 16.

A garden party with lanterns and balloons. Lots of guests and loud music.

Magic in the air☺.

My mom and John would be thrilled if I had a great party, like any other normal teenager.

But who am I kidding?

So, I decided to settle for cake and tea with my family.

My broken elbow is better now. Yesterday, I got the cast taken off, but my fingers still hurt when I write because I haven't used my hand for a long time☹.

How did I break my elbow?

Well, six weeks ago, we were at my Aunt Lise's birthday. Cousin Jon—the big fool—asked me to dance. I told him it was too risky, but he insisted.

"Oh, cut it out, it's just one dance," he laughed as he pulled me onto the dance floor, like a cow dragged off to the slaughter. And voilà. The first time he twirled me around, there was a loud crack in my elbow!

Result: My right elbow was broken in two places—six weeks in a cast.

The mailman just came.

A WHITE iPHONE—YES!

Ullerslev, 25 June 2017

Dear Diary,

I'm sorry for not writing sooner, but I have been quite busy. Guess what? I had another accident.

Again☹.

I wasn't really planning to go to the party, but for once Beate wanted to go, so…

Teachers are always present at these parties. They supervise and make sure that we don't spike the drinks.

But they don't see what's going on outside the school.

Or in the bathroom stalls!

Anyway, Nanna wanted us all to try Zumba, which she had learned on vacation in Spain. It looked like a lot of fun. They were all laughing. Then I had the brilliant idea to try, just this once. Of course, I would be very careful.

I was lucky.

I got away with only a brace on my arm.

Ullerslev, 11 July 2017

Dear Diary,

I had my usual note excusing me from PE. The others were playing basketball. My daring attempt to kick a runaway ball back to the court cost me a broken ankle.

At this point, you might have guessed that something is wrong with me. What keeps happening to me is not normal☹.

The doctors suspect it might be osteoporosis, a disease that weakens your bones. However, it's mostly older people that get that disease. I'm only 16. So, it's totally weird.

But that's how it is.

My bones just aren't strong enough. They snap at the slightest strain.

But why can't I just be careful?

Avoid sports and any sudden movements.

Not knowing exactly what's wrong with me, the doctors fear that it will only get worse.

So…I've sort of become part of the medical establishment.

We try and test everything the doctors can come up with.

Everyone's hoping to find a solution—especially me!

At school, the other kids call me 'the girl made of glass'
when they think I can't hear them☹.

Chapter 2
Life as I Know it

Ullerslev, 13 August 2017

Dear Diary,

Due to my condition, my life is not like that of other teenagers. It goes without saying that sports and dancing are off limits, because even the smallest impact can easily cause injury. I always have to think carefully about what I do. And preferably BEFORE I do it☺.

Therefore, I tend to settle for reading books and watching movies with my friends. And, of course, writing in my diary with my super-cool and super-expensive ballpoint pen.

Actually 'friends', the plural, is an exaggeration. Strictly speaking, I only have Beate!

We have known each other forever. She lives with her mom, dad and older brother in a house just a few streets away.

Beate is the greatest. She's smart—scores top marks in all the subjects. And she is beautiful, with bright blue eyes and golden hair. However, just like Lady Gaga, Beate is absolutely one of a kind. She only wears black clothes, preferably second-hand ones. From time to time, she dyes her hair wild colors. Last time she dyed it, her hair was bright neon yellow, and the time before that it was purple, and before that I think it was green. She also has piercings in her eyebrows.

She did them herself.

With a sewing needle!

Yuck!

Her parents freaked out. Normally, it takes a lot to get them angry, but for the piercings they really went ballistic. Following the incident Beate came over and spent a couple of days brooding in my room.

And me?

Well, my style is quite different. I dress in all colors and I don't care much for piercings or the Goth style.

In school I'm pretty average, I'm sorry to say, but I think it's due to my condition. I've missed a lot of classes☹.

Especially during these last few years.

As I said, Beate is super cool. Nobody could wish for a better friend. But, to be honest, and I guess that's the point of a diary, even though I have a best friend, I get a bit sad and lonely sometimes☹.

When I was eight, my dad died. He was a Native American. His family belongs to the Passamaquoddy tribe, a part of the Abenaki people. I have inherited my brown skin, dark eyes and shiny black hair from him. Naturally, being half Indian I look very different from the other kids in our little suburban town.

It is terrible to lose a parent and, following the loss, I isolated myself from the world. The only people I let in were my mom and Beate. My Indian looks, combined with Beate's provocative Goth style, means that we stand out in the crowd like sticks in the mud, and maybe somewhere along the way we became…well—sticks ☹.

I once asked Beate how she felt about us being different from the other kids. She stared at me as if I was from outer space.

"I don't want to be like everyone else," she said. "What would be the point of living the lives of dull, average people?"

Don't get me wrong—the others don't bully us. No. They smile and they talk kindly to us.

We are just not part of any close-knit group.

But can you blame them?

Who wants to spend time with someone who can't do anything without being picked up by an ambulance?

It's not as if I dream of being in a group. I don't even think I'm a pack animal. Sometimes I wonder though, if it would be nice to just blend in with the crowd. To be the *mud instead of the stick* ☹.

Just once in a while.

Victoria threw the diary on the floor. She was relieved that they had finally taken the cast off her left foot that morning. There was a pale patch on her leg where the skin had been concealed from the sun.

Six weeks ago, she had been at the bottom of the garden when a silvery-blue Mercedes stopped in front of number five. The house had been empty and up for sale for a long time, so Victoria had been curious to see who it was. A man stepped out of the car. It was a dark-skinned man with slick, black hair, dressed in a light-colored suit. He stamped the ground hard as if his feet were asleep. Victoria imagined that he had been on a long journey. Then another car arrived, and it too parked outside number five. The driver was holding a long, red sticker. He walked up to the sign that had almost become a permanent part of number five's front yard. He stuck the sticker on the sign.

Now, instead of FOR SALE, the sign read SOLD.

The real estate agent shook the dark-skinned man's hand, and they both looked very pleased.

Victoria had been absorbed in this little scene when the mailman arrived.

She caught sight of him moving toward her house, and she ran across the garden, curious to see if he had a letter from Beate, who was on holiday with her family. Beate, of course, wouldn't dream of sending an e-mail or a text message like everyone else. She only sent letters by mail. Many pages painstakingly printed with letters in blood-red ink. That was Beate's trademark.

One year, when Victoria's dad had still been alive, their families had gone on holiday to Canada together, and George had shown them the beautiful places of his ancestral home. Beate's parents had been overwhelmed by the easy-going lifestyle, the great lakes and never-ending forests, and they had returned many times.

This year Beate's family had gone to Canada again.

The mailbox hung on the wall near the driveway. On her way there, Victoria had jumped over a garden gnome and landed awkwardly, breaking her left foot.

Now she pulled out Beate's letter again and quickly flipped to page four.

I think I have located your dad's family. On the south coast of New Brunswick there is a tribe that locals used to call 'the glass people'. There might be a connection there☺.

Victoria had saved the letter. The part about 'the

glass people' kept churning in her head. How strange, she thought. Her dad's family still lived in Canada. He died in a hunting accident. It happened while he was back home visiting his family. Like her, he too had frequently suffered freak injuries. Thinking of how her condition made active life completely impossible, it must have been even harder for him—as he was part of a hunting culture.

Her father had been away on a hunting trip when he disappeared. He was on his own and, when he didn't return, the police had searched high and low, because they didn't know where or when he had lost his way. The search was in vain and, in the end, the police had to write in their report that he had probably fallen into one of the big lakes or been killed by a wild animal.

As they never found his body, they couldn't have a real funeral. Instead, Victoria's grandparents held a traditional Passamaquoddy ceremony.

Victoria's mom brought Victoria for the ceremony, but even though Victoria was eight years old and quite capable of understanding the strange things taking place at the funeral, all she could remember today was many beautiful people dancing to the sad sound of a distant drum. She had turned the scenery into a fixed picture of her father, and of her Indian heritage.

After the funeral, Victoria lost contact with her grandparents. They didn't like flying, so they never came to visit. Victoria's mom didn't talk about them much either and she only called them on birthdays and at Christmas. When Victoria got older, she realized that her mom—unconsciously—blamed her grandparents for what had happened.

Her Aunt Ann made an effort to stop by when she made one of her rare trips to Europe, nevertheless the family ties had eventually frayed.

Two years after Victoria's dad had passed away, her mom met John at the house of some friends. After a year, he moved in with them. John recognized and accepted that they needed space to grieve for Victoria's dad. In his own quiet way, he managed to be there for both Victoria and her mom.

Victoria looked at a yellowing sketch that Beate had included with the letter. She had bought it at a small market in a city called Saint John. In the sketch, a young Indian man was floating above a jagged cliff in a glade. Other Indians were lying scattered on the ground. It looked as if they were dead. Behind the cliff, the full moon gleamed, and it was reflected in the still, dark waters.

At the touch of the button, the computer lit up instantly.

Waiting to connect to the Internet, she looked out the window where a field of pink flowers peeped out among the greenery. When they had moved into this house in Ullerslev, her mom had created an English garden. Mom had a fondness for England because she had spent a year in London when she was young. This was where she had met Victoria's dad, at a party. It was love at first sight.

Victoria turned her attention back to the screen. She typed in 'Passamaquoddy'.

According to Google the tribe had a website of their own. She clicked on it. A page came up that said that they had lived in the northern part of Maine and Canadian New Brunswick. She also discovered a web-page concerning the rituals and legends of the Passamaquoddy tribe.

After a few more clicks, she got caught up in one of their fascinating stories. It was about the mighty thunderbirds, which were considered the source of thunder and lightning. Like Thor in Norse mythology. But the thunderbirds were not gods like Thor. They were chosen Indians who put on wings and flew about, creating thunder.

One day, a young Indian wanted to know where the thunder came from. He journeyed off and found a tribe in the mountains that knew the answer to his question. To show him the origin of thunder, the elders of the tribe crushed every bone in his body. Then, they reshaped him in the spirit of a thunderbird by giving him a magic potion that gave him great strength and restored his mobility. He grew wings and flew off with the other thunderbirds.

'I can easily imagine what it must have felt like when all his bones were broken,' thought Victoria.

She turned off the computer, put on a T-shirt and went to bed.

Chapter 3
The Mad Doctor

IN HER DREAM, she floated in mid-air, 15 feet above the cliff in the sketch from Beate's letter. She could hear a swishing sound behind her. She was weightless, and therefore it was impossible for her to swing around to see what it was. Unable to maneuver she slipped quietly through the air toward some tall, dark trees surrounding a glade.

When she neared the trees, the swishing sound increased. At the end, it sounded like a warning— don't get too close to the trees. She tried to fight it, but it was no use. She floated right into the shade of the tall trees and the darkness swallowed her....

"Noooo!" Victoria sat up in bed, startled. She looked around frantically. It took her a moment to realize that she was in her room, and that it had all been a dream.

She let herself fall backward onto her pillow. It was soaked in sweat. "Yuck!"

It had to be early morning. Although some light peeked through the blinds, she didn't hear any birds.

During the night, her duvet had fallen on the floor. She got up and threw it back onto the bed.

She walked over to the window and the blind flicked up when she released the cord. She pushed the window open. The cool air slowly brought her back from her dreamlike state.

She looked at the old apple tree in the garden and it made her think of the tall dark trees in her dream. It had certainly been a bizarre nightmare. The cliff had been identical to the one in Beate's sketch. It was impossible to mistake its strange shape.

Why was she dreaming of trees and a rocky cliff?

She couldn't shake the ominous feeling that the dream had been a warning!

She still felt uneasy when she sat down in front of the computer. She typed 'thunderbirds' into the Google search box. Would she maybe be able to find something about that magic potion?

The search offered no useful results. After another few searches of 'Passamaquoddy' combined with 'medicine man', she found a story about the first medicine man of the Passamaquoddy tribe. As a baby, he had been sailing down the river in a small basket. The Indians found him between the reeds and took him in. They had no idea that he was a magical being.

To make sure the tribe would keep him, a poor motherless child, he had secretly killed off several of the tribe's other children. When he became an adult, he felt remorse. He couldn't undo what he had done, so instead he decided to put his knowledge of medicine and magic to use for the good of the tribe. To prove to them that he would never go back on his word, he ripped every bone out of his body. This way he was no longer able to move and had to spend all his time in his tent—patiently waiting for his tribesmen to require his assistance.

Victoria turned off the computer. She was puzzled. In most of the fairytales she knew, the hero had to manage three challenges to win the princess. To the Indians, the road to greatness seemed to involve severe bodily pain and agony. Managing three challenges just wasn't enough. To prepare him for his mission, the hero also had to have his body dismembered!

It was rather daunting.

* * *

The next day her mother got a phone call from one of their doctors at Rigshospitalet. He suggested that they got in contact with a clinic in Germany specializing in bone diseases.

Victoria had undergone numerous medical examinations and tests due to her condition and, so far, none of them had produced any significant or definitive results. Victoria's mother and John didn't need much time to consider the doctor's proposal.

"I can take some time off work," Victoria's mom said. Then she called the German clinic and made an appointment.

The clinic was located in Dresden, in the southeast corner of former East Germany, and one week later Victoria and her mom made the almost eighthour drive to the clinic. At the clinic, Doctor Dederich Schwartz received them. He was in his mid-forties, dark haired, with high cheekbones and pale, almost greyish skin.

As soon as they had arrived, he started performing a series of tests.

Dresden, 8 October 2017

Dear Diary,

I have undergone heaps of tests! Today I had to do some physical exercises. I don't exactly know what they were for, but afterward they did a whole lot of measurements. As always, Mom was keen to show solidarity and insisted on doing the exercises with me. I think we must have done at least a thousand repetitions of all sorts. It was tough. Like me, she is not exactly in good shape, and we were sweating buckets☺.

Anyway, apart from that, it's not so bad here in Dresden.

The rooms are nice and the food is great. The other patients are all older people, but that figures☺.

They're all nice to me, and I get to practice my German. The stay might even improve my chance of surviving next year's German exam.

The only problem is Dr Schwartz.

His small pig-like eyes keep following me everywhere I go, and I keep getting the feeling that there's something he's keeping from us!

He performs all those tests and yet he seems strangely content with his apparent lack of findings.

He's acting weird and I don't like him☹.

It was their last day in Dresden. Victoria and her mom were in Victoria's room. They were waiting for Dr Schwartz to come by with his final report and sign her out, so that they could get started on their long drive back to Denmark. As far as they could tell, none of the tests had revealed any useful information about Victoria's disease.

"I'm afraid this has been a total waste of time," Victoria's mother sighed.

"Yes, a waste of time and money," Victoria agreed. Finally, at five o'clock, there was a knock on the door. Dr Schwartz stepped in. He made himself comfortable at the table and carefully stacked a small pile of documents in front of him. He fiddled with the top buttons of his coat, and then he turned to Victoria.

His stare made Victoria feel uncomfortable.

"You're of Indian descent, aren't you?"

Victoria nodded.

"Where are you from?"

"My dad's family lives in New Brunswick. It's in the eastern part of Canada."

The doctor snorted. "I thought so—perhaps the Abenaki people?"

"Yes, the Passamaquoddy tribe."

"And your dad, where is he?" the doctor asked.

"I really can't see why this is of any relevance," Victoria's mother interrupted. Her lips had tightened in a dark straight line and a faint red blush was coloring her cheeks.

Victoria knew her mother well enough to know that a storm was brewing.

Dr Schwartz did not respond, but he looked at her contemptuously. He produced a small vial from his pocket and placed it on the table. It was not much bigger than a thimble.

"I would like to try something," he said, and pushed it toward Victoria.

Victoria picked up the small vial.

"What is it?" her mom asked.

"It's the stuff that dreams are made of!" The doctor laughed in a strangely squeaky way.

"But what's in it?" Victoria's mother insisted. "I need to know what it is, if you want Victoria to test it."

By the way her mother sneered the word 'test', Victoria could tell that the storm was just about to hit the shore.

"Mostly herbs and seeds. It's entirely natural stuff, I can assure you. I think it's time to try alternative medicine," he said, in a begrudging tone of voice.

Victoria turned to her mother for approval. "Natural medicine. I guess it can't hurt?" she said.

Victoria's mom hesitated. "I don't see the point," she finally said. "We've been here for more than a week and in ten minutes we are going home. I think it's a bit late to test a new treatment."

Dr Schwartz jumped up, "But that's the beauty of it. With this medicine, we will know immediately if it has any effect!" His eyes widened when Victoria's mom got up and reached for her bag.

"SIT DOWN!" he almost yelled, and he pointed at her chair. "I'm sure this will work!"

Victoria's mom raised her voice. "We both know it isn't possible!"

"You're a fool if you don't believe me!" Dr Schwartz yelled.

"Are you calling me a fool?"

"No," Dr Schwartz answered hastily. "What I mean is that…"

"STOP, both of you!" Victoria cut in. She looked at her mom. "What if he's right? Let me at least try it!"

For several seconds her mother seemed to be fighting an inner battle. Then Victoria's pleading face made her give in. "Okay then."

Victoria removed the cork from the vial and smelled the mixture. There was a vague scent of something familiar, but she couldn't quite put her finger on it. Then she poured the thick mixture onto her tongue and swallowed. At first, nothing happened. Then a slow heat started spreading through her body. It began in her stomach, and moved into her arms and legs. The heat increased, and colored her cheeks. It made her feel dizzy, but then the heat subsided, leaving her pleasantly warm and relaxed. Her cheeks changed from a flushed red to an almost golden glow.

It seemed to Victoria that Dr Schwartz's face lit up with passion when she looked at him. He got up, walked around the table and gave Victoria a shove!

She fell off her seat and knocked her shoulder hard against the wall.

"How dare you?" Her mom jumped up to help her.

Victoria was on the floor, curled up against the wall. While trying to assess the damage to her body, she carefully pushed herself up into a sitting position. Instead of giving her shooting pains, the movement sent her flying from the floor. She landed like a cat all the way over by the door.

"YEEES!" laughed Dr Schwartz. "I knew it!" He pranced around the room triumphantly.

"You're crazy!" Victoria's mom yelled, and she waved her fist at the doctor. Then she turned to Victoria and eased her into an armchair. "Are you okay?"

Victoria heard the question, but did not respond. She felt absorbed by the almost explosive energy pulsating through her body.

Her vision was acute. Looking through the window, she could clearly see the veins of even the smallest leaves on a tree in the distance. The humming of bees buzzing about in some flower bushes in the garden sounded like a helicopter lifting off.

"You must see the elders of my chapter immediately!" the doctor said excitedly.

"No! We are leaving right now!" Victoria's mom was furious.

"But it is really important that they see you! That you meet.... It's essential for all of us!" he stuttered.

"What is wrong with you? I should report this to the police!" Victoria's mom cried.

"But it worked! Nothing happened to her!" he pleaded.

"But you didn't know that! Something awful could have happened to her! We've undergone all your experiments, and seen no results of any kind. Then you force some strange potion on us, and, on top of that, you push her into the wall! We're leaving. Get out of our way!" The storm had arrived. Like a tigress protecting her cubs, she got in between Dr Schwartz and her daughter.

Ready to fight.

For a second he hesitated, then he stepped aside. Victoria's mom turned around and, with a firm grip on Victoria's shoulder, she aimed for the door.

"My bag!" cried Victoria and tore herself away from her mother. She ran to get her bag, which was resting on the bed.

Dr Schwartz reached out frantically, and caught her arm. "No. No, I said. You're staying here!"

Much to Victoria's surprise, she brushed away his hand as if it was nothing more than a butterfly resting on her arm.

"It's really, really important... You have to work with us!" he screamed. "Work with us.... Work with US!"

They heard him chanting the same sentence over and over again, until the elevator door closed behind them. On the lower floor, they hurried to Victoria's mom's room to get her luggage.

Then they left the clinic through the large glass

doors, and found the parking lot where they had parked their Ford Focus. After a detour through a small park in the dim evening light, they managed to find the highway.

They did not see the dark car that followed them north throughout the night, toward the Danish border.

On board the ferry, Victoria solved a five-star Sudoku in just one minute!

When they rolled into the driveway the next morning, Victoria carried both their bags and two crates of duty-free soft drinks into the house with unusual ease.

"My goodness," Victoria's mom yelled. "Put down the crates, before you get hurt!"

When John heard about the doctor's highly unprofessional behavior, he was shocked.

"But the potion had a remarkable effect on me," Victoria explained. "I got super hearing and my vision…all my senses were sharpened! I even got strong, like Hercules."

But to Victoria's surprise, and huge disappointment, John and her mom both thought that the effect of the potion was bogus. A placebo effect at best. Probably amplified by the need Victoria felt for a quick fix after spending more than a week at the clinic. John agreed with Victoria's mom's conclusion completely. The trip had been nothing but a waste of time.

* * *

After lunch, Victoria went to her room. The warm feeling from the potion had worn off. All of a sudden, she felt drained. She lay down on her couch. Somehow, she felt slightly disappointed. Despite John and her mom's beliefs, the potion HAD worked a miracle!

If they had stayed at the clinic, she might have had the chance to test it some more.

But then again, the mere thought of Dr Dederich Schwartz made her feel ill at ease, and that final scene had convinced her that there was something fishy about the whole thing.

What was it he had said? He wanted her to meet the elders of his chapter.

Chapter?

It didn't make sense.

She got up, turned on the computer and looked up 'chapter' on the Internet. Not surprisingly, the word was mostly used in books, but she also found an article about the early days of Christianity where every convent had its own order and the various tiers of the hierarchy were called chapters. It was a type of group definition.

The Knights Templar had also been divided into chapters. Then she realized that, in a way, the same went for Indians. The Indian nations were also divided into smaller tribes. For instance, her father's own tribe, the Passamaquoddy, was a sub-section of the Abenaki people.

Just before the doctor gave her the potion, he had asked if she was Abenaki. How could he have known?

Was he also of Indian descent?

Chapter 4
Big Plans

VICTORIA CALLED BEATE. Victoria was so excited that the words came out in incoherent fragments, and the conversation did not make much sense to Beate. In the end, Beate said she was coming over.

When Beate arrived, Victoria was at her desk. The computer screen was the only light source in the dark room. Old dictionaries and history books were scattered everywhere, and Beate had to turn on the ceiling light before it was safe to cross the floor.

Annoyed by the disruption and half blinded by the light, Victoria swung her office chair around. Then she saw that it was Beate.

"Isn't it *awesome*?" Victoria said.

"Hmm, so it was a good trip to Germany. What did the doctors say?" Beate asked, while she cleared the old armchair that Victoria had bought at a garage sale.

"I told you on the phone!" Victoria cried out. Then she shook her head. "You're not going to believe this...."

When Victoria finished telling the story about the doctor and the potion, she threw her arms in the air.

"It's a wonder drug—just imagine.... I don't know if it can cure me entirely, but at least it works for a while. It even gave me supernatural strength. I was so cool!"

"Great. That's fantastic. So where do you get this potion? At the pharmacy? Or is it something you have to order on some website for mad doctors and voodoo witches?" asked Beate.

Victoria laughed.

"That's the problem! The creepy doctor didn't say what it was. He just said it was a natural product. And I can't just call and ask him, can I? Not after we left like that. Besides, I don't think he would tell me anyways. He seemed very secretive. I don't know what's going on but at least we know that the potion exists, and that the effect is pure Asterix and Obelix."

"And just because you fell into the caldron as a child, the mad Druid Getafix won't let you have any more of his magic potion," Beate moaned in her best Gaulish accent, feigning resentment.

"Oh stop it, Beate. It's not funny. Really! I was as strong as Obelix, and all my senses were sharpened to a level you can't imagine. I could see the lines in a leaf of a tree a hundred yards away. I could hear every word uttered on the floor above me!"

"But why did he give it to you then? Why didn't

he drink it himself?"

"Well, that's a really good question. Even though he was the one who had the drug, he seemed surprisingly curious to see what effect it would have on me. So your guess is as good as mine!" Victoria said. She clapped her hands. "Will you help me find out more?"

"Don't I always?" Beate said with a grin.

"Yes, you do. And I really appreciate it. Listen up then! I've checked all the reference books in the house. Guess what I found? Nothing!" She got up. "Now I'm going to get John's laptop, so we can both search the Internet at the same time. Do you understand what we're looking for?"

"Yeah, yeah, secret recipes for magic potions."

Victoria smiled.

"Let's go!"

The bluish gleam of the two screens battled the shadows of the room until the morning sun cast rays of light across the table and they turned off their computers. Their efforts had been in vain. They had not found anything that seemed to relate to the mysterious potion. Beate pulled out her mattress from underneath Victoria's bed. A mattress she had won the right to consider her own a long time ago. They fell asleep to the sound of the early birds chirping.

* * *

"What did it taste like?"

"It didn't taste like anything I've ever had before. It was a dark green porridge in a small vial the size of a thimble," Victoria answered.

"But you must remember something." Beate picked distractedly at her right eyebrow, now pierced with no less than three small silver rings. "Was it bark-like?"

"How would I know? I don't know what bark tastes like!"

"We REALLY need something to go on. At least one ingredient. Otherwise it's hopeless! I've found a recipe for bark soup! Only natural ingredients, bark and fresh insects—yuck. That sounds so gross, I sincerely hope it's not what we're looking for. So Victoria, did it have bark in it?"

Victoria thought Beate's voice sounded a bit agitated. She shook her head.

"No, I don't think it had bark in it."

* * *

"Could cabbage, maybe, be one of the ingredients?"

It had been a whole week since Victoria returned from Dresden. They had found nothing that could point them in the direction of what the strange potion was made of.

"I've said it a hundred times. It was a weird blend that could contain just about anything. But no, there was no distinct hint of cabbage."

"Well, the cabbage butterfly caterpillars in this stew will be glad to hear that!" Beate laughed.

She puffed up her cheeks to look like a caterpillar. "Listen." She put on a serious face, "Couldn't we, just for a moment, consider calling Dr Schwartz? We have been cooped up in your room for a week now, and we still don't have a single clue!"

Victoria automatically started shaking her head.

"Please, please," Beate begged her. "We're wasting our youth in here."

Finally Victoria gave in. "Alright, I'll call him. But I don't have a good feeling about it. Not at all. He was so creepy!"

Victoria got up. In the desk drawer, she found her papers from the clinic in Dresden. Halfway through dialing the number, she paused. "I don't..."

"DIAL!" Beate was not letting her off the hook. "If you want the potion, you call him!"

Victoria finished dialing the number.

"Dr Dederich Schwartz," a voice said on the speakerphone.

"Hello, this is Victoria Han..."

"VICTORIA! Where are you? I mean, it's so good of you to call, I have been thinking about you. What happened? You left in such a hurry!"

Victoria looked at Beate.

"He sounds okay, I think," Beate shrugged her shoulders.

"We didn't understand what you wanted from us," Victoria felt nauseous confronting him.

"You wouldn't let us go!"

The phone was quiet for a second.

"And we still need to do some more tests! If I'm right, the elders will want to meet you. It's a great honor, and you will live here and serve the brotherhood!"

This time Beate looked at Victoria.

"Maybe he really is crazy!" she whispered.

Victoria cleared her throat. "What's in the potion? Where did you get it?"

"The brothers made it, following the instructions from the old chief. Just like the legend describes! Do you want me to come get you? We can be back at the clinic in the morning!" Dr Schwartz' voice was rising with anticipation.

Victoria wanted to hang up. Just talking to him on the phone already felt too close. He was unstable.

Under no circumstances could he come here.

What would he do if they met again?

"Is the recipe described in the legends?" she asked.

"The recipe IS the legend," he said.

"What does that have to do with me?" Victoria asked.

"The elders will be thrilled, and I will be famous," he said. "And you can help me validate my research!"

Victoria hit the small red phone icon and threw the phone on the bed.

She turned to Beate. "See? I told you he was mad!"

"You win!" Beate sighed.

"And you're still with me on this one?" Victoria said.

"But it's really boring!" said Beate.

"I know, but if we identify the potion, I can become just as normal as you, and everyone else. I can have a life with parties, sports and boyfriends."

Beate looked offended. "Normal? Me? You don't have to go to that extreme.... Even if the bit about boyfriends does sound good!"

"I promise never to utter such nonsense again," Victoria laughed and crossed her heart.

"Okay, I will help you. Have I ever let you down?"

"You're the best. Back to googling then!"

* * *

They also scoured the shelves of the public library for just about anything on Indians and their legends. They even took some Indian cookbooks home. Victoria picked up one of them. It contained recipes originating from some of the Indian ceremonial gatherings. Victoria noticed that the publishing house that had printed the book also had a website. On the website, she found another version of the legend of the thunderbirds.

After talking to Dr Schwartz, Victoria was pretty convinced that the magic potion was the one mentioned when the young Indian has his bones crushed and was 'reassembled' by the elders. The potion gave the Indian great power, the same power that she had gotten at the clinic. So far, there had been no mention of the ingredients though.

In the corner of the screen was a 'home' icon. She clicked it, and a new page opened. It was the website of an amateur historian named Mary Joan Steward.

Suddenly Beate threw her arms in the air. "Look at this map! There is an entire area called Passamaquoddy Bay and even a national park called Quoddy Head." Beate pointed to a tiny speck near the US–Canadian border. "It obviously has something to do with your dad's tribe. And look there, a visitors' center. I wonder what they have to offer a tourist in the middle of nowhere…."

Victoria sat down on the floor next to Beate. She studied the awkward map on the screen.

"Try clicking the link to the visitor center's homepage," Victoria suggested.

Beate clicked, and for a second they watched the page reload.

"It's a page on Mary Joan Steward's website!" said Victoria.

Beate looked puzzled.

Along the left side of the screen were some small, titled photos, probably from various events that had taken place.

Beate clicked on the latest folder, 'Spiritual gathering, summer 2017.'

More photos appeared, of both Indians and European-looking people standing between some huts on the edge of a forest.

Some of the photos were too dark to see. They were photos taken outside at dusk. Indistinctive silhouettes, trees and cliffs.

"It's like in the sketch!" exclaimed Victoria.

She pulled the laptop away from Beate.

"What sketch?" Beate said.

"The one you sent me from Canada!"

Beate took a closer look at the picture. "Oh yes, I remember. I bought it in a market where they sold all sorts of old stuff. It was in Saint John, a nice city by the sea." She clicked back and studied the map carefully. "Actually it looks like Saint John might not be that far away from Quoddy Head." She pointed to the screen. "I bought the sketch because the woman in the market stall said it was Passamaquoddy and she called them the Glasspeople."

"Maybe, but nevertheless it all fits. We have to go there!" said Victoria.

"Go there? What do you mean? Go to Canada?"

"Yes, don't you see! My dad's family, the photos, the potion and the legends. It all fits. First, I have to talk to that Mary Joan woman at the visitors' center and…and…"

Beate placed a hand on Victoria's arm.

"There's nothing I would rather do than go with you, but what will our parents say? Canada? It's hard enough to get their permission for a daytrip to Copenhagen!"

Victoria dropped her head. "You're right, but I just know that the key to it all is waiting for us right there!"

"Hey, don't worry, we'll find a way. We just have to plan this carefully. First, we have to find an explanation as to why we suddenly have to go to New Brunswick. It's probably not a good idea to tell them about those thunderbirds. Or the potion. They'll think we've lost it. Or at least that you have!" Beate laughed.

"My grandparents live in Pennfield. That's in New Brunswick. Maybe it isn't far from Quoddy Head and the visitors' center. How big can these provinces be?"

"Let's go see your grandparents then!" Beate beamed.

"I haven't seen them since my dad died. My mom is afraid that their way of living might kill me off too. There is no way that she will let me go see them!"

"Really? Canada is perfectly safe. Roads, hot running water, electricity. Let's have some tea and figure out our next move." They went to the kitchen in search of tea and mugs.

"First, we have to convince my mom to allow us to visit my grandparents. And then there is the small issue of money." Victoria poured water into the kettle and opened up a cupboard to get a roll of cookies. She unwrapped the roll and stuck a whole cookie into her mouth before she placed the roll on a plate. "Let's go sit in the living room. Could you grab the mugs?" Victoria mumbled, her mouth full of crumbs.

"You could say that, now that you're older, you want to find your roots and you'd like to go to Canada to see where your dad grew up. And we can stay in Saint John, so they know you won't go native on them," Beate suggested. "I've been there remember? I know the city, and I recommend it!"

She sat down on the soft couch next to Victoria. With the laptop on one knee and a hot cup of tea balanced on the other, she opened up Mary Joan's website. "Maybe we could participate in her next event—the 'Christmas wing ding' on the 18 to the 21 December. That sounds like a perfect occasion!"

"Yes, you're right. It's perfect!" Victoria jumped up. Her arm knocked over Beate's mug and tea splashed onto the couch. Beate tried to close the laptop before the hot tea splashed it too, but she was too late.

"Easy now!" Beate exclaimed while she tried wiping up the spill with her sleeve.

"Sorry." Victoria grinned. "Flip it over so the tea doesn't seep into the keyboard!"

Beate quickly turned the laptop upside down. Victoria went to the kitchen and came back with some paper towels that she handed to Beate.

"Arhh, I have to go to the hospital in mid-December. I'm participating in yet another study to find out what's wrong with me. They'll give me a device that measures my blood. I have to test it twice a day during the Christmas break."

"I'm sure you can bring the device with you," Beate said.

"Yes, probably. But doing all these tests all the time makes me feel even sicker. I hate it!"

"Just look at the bright side. You get to go to Canada and your parents won't have to listen to you complaining about doing things you hate. It's a win-win!" Beate said with a smirk. "That just leaves my parents, but they owe me. Since freshman year I have kept expressing myself to a minimum.... They literally begged me! Now it's time to cash in!" Beate said, with a sly little smile on her lips.

* * *

"No!" said her mom, without hesitating.

"No?"

"You know what happened to your dad. Canada is a wilderness, and your family being Native American doesn't make it any safer. And what about your condition? You know we have to do those tests, and besides it's icy cold over there! You might fall and break something!"

John ended up saving the day. "Julie, you have to let her grow up. The family in Canada is part of her too and it's high time she visit her grandparents again," he said. "It would be terrible if they lost contact forever."

"It has been almost ten years since I last saw them," Victoria added, to support the argument. "And Beate has been to Canada several times. It's civilized. They live in houses and have electricity and everything!"

"Don't be silly," her mom said, but Victoria could tell that she felt a little guilty.

"I'm sure Auntie Ann will pick me up at the airport, so I don't even have to take the bus," Victoria argued.

"But what if you break something?"

"They have hospitals there too, you know."

"Of course they do…" her mom said. "But…"

"Let her go," John interrupted. "She's 16 and you need to let go. She'll be alright and they'll take good care of her."

Victoria's mom gave in. "Since it's two against one…I'll call your grandparents. They'll be happy to see you."

Victoria gave her mom a big hug. "Can Beate come to? She's dying to come along, and I'm sure she can stay with Fione and Charles too. They live in an enormous house!"

"Well…" her mother said, "I'll have to ask Charles and Fione obviously, but I can't imagine they would say no."

* * *

Charles and Fione were thrilled that Victoria wanted to visit, and of course she could bring Beate.

When Fi hung up, she turned to her husband.

"Victoria is coming to visit us for Christmas," she said, with tears in her eyes.

"How wonderful," said Charles, taking her by the hand.

"But her osteoporosis has gotten worse. It's very strange that, out of all the people in the world, our young granddaughter should suffer from such a cruel bone disease."

Charles' smile faded. "Fate is unpredictable," he said, clutching her hand.

"But she can't be the one," Fi said. Her voice was trembling.

"No, of course not." Charles agreed. "She's a girl!"

However, for a brief moment Fi thought she spotted a shadow of doubt in his eyes.

Chapter 5
New Neighbors

THE SOUND OF HEAVY TRAFFIC woke Victoria. Still half asleep, she drew the curtain aside and winced against the sunlight. What was that noise? Her neighborhood was usually so quiet.

Several large trucks passed by in the street. They went slowly, as if they couldn't find their way. Then they stopped. Right outside number five. Maybe the new owners were moving in?

She showered, and grabbed a pair of jeans and a T-shirt. She hurried through the living room and out the front door.

The trucks were still parked outside the empty house. A lot of people were busy unloading.

Victoria crossed the street and hid in the shade of some tall lilacs outside number five. From there she could watch what was going on unnoticed. People carried boxes and furniture to the house. They also hauled outdoor furniture around to the back garden, where a couple of men were busy putting up a large, white party tent.

"Do you live around here?"

Victoria jumped in surprise. She turned to see a girl, also hiding in the shade, but on the other side of the peeling fence. Had she been there all along? Victoria had not noticed her arrival.

"Yes, I live just across the street—in number eight. The white house. You have a lot of people moving for you!"

The girl flashed a wide smile. She was beautiful, and about Victoria's age. Tanned, with curly, dark, almost black hair.

"We're a big family alright. At times, it almost gets too crowded with all these uncles, aunts and cousins," she shrugged. "But of course, it also comes in handy sometimes."

"Like on moving day?" Victoria laughed.

"Oh yes, it's definitely an advantage when you have to move." The girl smiled again. "I'm Sarah."

"I'm Victoria."

"Pleased to meet you, Victoria. Won't you come inside and meet the family?" She flashed another gleaming smile.

Victoria nodded and followed her inside.

The uncles, cousins and other family

members moving things around in the garden looked kindly at her, but otherwise didn't seem to pay her much attention. Out of the shade, Victoria could see that they all had black hair and brown skin, just like her.

"Where are you from?" Victoria asked.

"We've just moved from North Zealand, but originally our family came from Romania. These days though, we live all over Europe. I have family in Ireland, England, France, Italy and Germany."

"So are you going to live here, or are you just helping out?"

Sarah smiled. "I'm moving in. Me, my parents and my brother, that is. The others are just lending a hand—and later they're here for a party. This year is our turn to host the annual get-together of *die ganze klan*," she laughed. It sounded funny when she said *ganze*.

"This way we get settled in no time. The party is tomorrow, and everybody will make damn sure everything is ready!" she said.

Victoria laughed, "Good point—nobody in their right mind will want to miss out on a party!"

A woman wearing a bright orange scarf around her head waved to them from a first floor window.

"That's my mom!" Sarah waved back. "Come on, I'll show you around."

Victoria followed her. Sarah's jacket was open, and underneath she wore a light blue, button-down shirt. On the collar was a large brooch. It looked like an oversized pin with a white mother of pearl pinhead. Victoria thought that it was an unusual piece of jewelry for a girl that age. It was something more suitable for a grandmother.

Then, a young man caught Victoria's eye.

He was leaning against the wall with his arms crossed in front of him. He looked directly at Victoria. A small smile pulled at the corner of his mouth. He was muscular, with narrow hips. His hair was black and his features gentle. He straightened up as their eyes met.

He was the most handsome guy Victoria had ever seen.

Making eye contact made her heart beat faster but, at the same time, there was something about his confident smile that made her feel uneasy.

"That's Roberto. My older brother," Sarah said, without even looking in his direction. "Come on, let's go inside."

Suddenly, it was as if a grey cloud shaded the sun.

Everything went still.

Victoria felt as if all the movement in the garden had frozen.

As if all the attention was focused on her.

"Thanks, but I better be getting home," she mumbled. She forced herself to look away from Roberto's dark eyes.

Victoria turned around, but Sarah grabbed hold of her arm.

"Come on, just for a minute!" Sarah's grip was not tight, yet it held Victoria back.

Victoria shook her head. Immediately she felt a shooting pain in her right shoulder. The pain traveled down her arm and across her chest, for a moment she felt faint. She tried hard to collect her thoughts. Then everything returned to normal.

"Ouch!" Victoria pulled away and headed for the gate. She just wanted to get home.

"Another time then!" Sarah called out behind her, while Victoria half ran into the street. She didn't look back to see if Sarah was following her.

An insect must have stung her. If it was a bee, she would need an antidote straight away. Last time she was stung by a bee, her thigh was swollen for days. As a shortcut, Victoria jumped over the gutter that ran along the street and slipped through the beech hedge into her back garden. As she pushed through the hedge, a branch caught the front pocket of her otherwise tight jeans. She swirled around to pull free but fell and twisted her left foot.

Sarah stood in the doorway until Victoria was out of sight. Then she turned around and went into the house. In her hand she held the brooch. The pinhead was no longer white.

It was blood red.

Chapter 6
Canada

ON THE FLIGHT FROM Paris to Montreal, Beate practiced her French on a young man sitting across the aisle. He was very susceptible to the beautiful Danish girl when she approached him, and the two of them ended up talking during the whole flight. When they left the plane, he and Beate exchanged addresses and promised to keep in touch.

"This trip really got off to a perfect start," Beate beamed, when they were waiting at the baggage carousel. "He was very charming and clever too. Just my kind of guy."

From Quebec, they took a small, twin-engine plane with only ten passengers on board. When they arrived at Saint John's International Airport, Ann was there waiting.

"There you are!" Auntie Ann shouted from a distance. She ran toward Victoria and embraced her heartily. "It's so wonderful to see you again. And your friend!" she said, and gave Beate a warm hug as well.

The family resemblance was striking and Victoria could not take her eyes off Ann.

Aunt Ann had the same arched nose, although it

was not quite as pointy as her brother's had been. Her long, black hair was shiny, and she had an attractive mouth with full-bodied lips. Ann was in her mid-forties, but had never married or had kids of her own.

"You are so beautiful!" Ann hugged her again and Victoria felt her own eyes tearing up as well.

"I am so happy to finally be here. And I am so excited to see Grandma and Grandpa again," Victoria said.

"I can assure you that they're waiting eagerly. Fi has called me a dozen times with all sorts of questions," Ann said, laughing, "wondering if maybe you would like corn pancakes, and if I think you're aware of how cold it is in Canada. They worry that you didn't pack enough warm clothes."

* * *

When they walked out of the airport and into the snowy parking lot, Victoria stopped and took a deep breath, taking in the frosty Canadian December night.

"We have a long drive ahead of us. If you're tired, you can just take a rest in the back," Ann said. They got into her black Range Rover, it was so spacious they could almost lie stretched out in the back seat.

The engine hummed quietly as they made their way west into the snowy landscape. Both girls were fast asleep before they reached the coast and the beautiful New River Beach, where even the sea was frozen and covered in snow.

Finally, they reached the dimly lit streets of Pennfield town. Despite being a four-wheel drive, the Range Rover skidded when they climbed the steep driveway to Fione and Charles' house late at night.

Fione, or Fi as she had been called ever since she was a little girl, had her silver-grey hair gathered in a bun. She wore an apron over her Indian dress. Her arched nose hinted at her inquisitive soul. Despite her gentle exterior, a fire burned in her eyes.

"I've been waiting for you to visit for so long!" Fi pulled Victoria close and held her in a long, firm embrace. Then she turned to Beate and bid her a warm welcome, too.

"First, let me show you the guest room," Charles said. "Then we'll talk."

Charles was tall, straight-backed and broad. His long, greying, dark hair was gathered into a ponytail. He, too, had a fire burning in his eyes. In contrast to his wife, he was dressed in Western clothes.

The guest bedroom was cozy. A bed lined each wall. The beds were made up with quilts and plenty of soft pillows and cushions in warm purple and orange colors.

The girls dropped their bags and hurried back down to the spacious kitchen with its rustic atmosphere.

Aunt Ann lived in Saint John, and the trip back through the snow would be long and hard. Therefore, she would spend the night and leave in the morning. She had also been assigned a bedroom in the large, three-story house.

"Now let's eat," Fi said. "You've had a long journey so you must be hungry."

Much to Beate's liking an open fire roared in the kitchen and, although it was the middle of the night, Fi had set the kitchen table with corn pancakes, vegetables, beans, and mugs of steaming hot tea. Fi brought out her knitting and sat by the table, smiling at them while they ate hungrily.

When their appetites had been satisfied, Charles said, "So, you finally decided to come visit your family."

"I've wanted to visit you for a long time, but it's a very long trip. I had to wait for my mom to agree that I was old enough to go on my own. She's very protective. And due to my illness, she's always concerned that I might hurt myself," Victoria explained.

Charles raised his eyebrows.

"Your mom warned us that your condition has

worsened in the last couple of years."

Victoria nodded.

She told them about her tests, the trip to Dresden and even the scary doctor, but she didn´t say anything about the potion since—in the general grown-up opinion expressed by both her mom and John—it was all in her head.

Fi placed her hand on Victoria's shoulder. "Ever since the doctors found out that you had inherited the dreadful disease, we have been so worried! I still remember the day your mother phoned and told us the news. It was only a short while after your father died," she said.

"It has been a hard time for us," Charles said, "but we're relieved that, in spite of everything, you are doing so well.... It didn't stop you from traveling and, now, here you are! Finally!" Her granddad looked so happy, and she leaned forward and gave him a kiss on the cheek.

When Victoria, Beate and Ann had gone upstairs to their rooms, Fi looked at her reflection in the dark kitchen windows. Even though this long-awaited visit from Denmark had been like a breath of fresh air, she suddenly felt the stillness of the dark night closing in on her.

* * *

Diane Southby looked at the long, slender needle. It had arrived by express airmail from Denmark with instructions regarding her next mission. Earlier tasks had been to blog and publish boring articles about Indian stuff on a certain website, and to show up at different events with other people from the site in order to infiltrate the Indian society.

Any idiot could have done it, but the elders had chosen her because some of her distant relatives had been Indian too.

Now she had finally been trusted with a real, important mission. She was to engage a girl and enroll her in the brotherhood. That was plan A.

However, if there were any problems, she had to take the girl out by stabbing her with the needle. That was plan B.

Diane picked up her tool of destruction and examined its red mother of pearl pinhead. She was puzzled. There was no way this tiny thing could do any serious harm to a human being. She bent over to carefully place the needle back on the table and felt her assault knife press against her skin—it was always tucked in at the back of her skirt inside her short jacket.

The outcome would be far more certain if she used the knife. However, the instructions were clear. Win her over or stab her with the needle. Perhaps it was symbolic or...some of that Carpathian mumbo jumbo.

Anyway, the elders didn't do anything without a perfectly good reason, and she would do as she was told!

Diane pressed 'send' on the e-mail signing her up for the Christmas wing ding. Once again, she would be leaving sunny Florida for some cold and snow-covered part of Canada!

Chapter 7
Mary Joan Steward

A SNOWSTORM WAS HOWLING outside, and it was almost lunchtime before the young visitors in the guestroom stirred. Their comfortable beds had been like padded nests protecting them from the cold of night.

Victoria ventured out of bed. "The floor is freezing," she cried and started dancing around in her underwear. Beate laughed when Victoria leapt back under the warm quilts.

It was high noon when the two girls finally got up and joined the others in the kitchen. Big snowplows had been busy since dawn, and, with the storm settling, the roads were now navigable. Charles had cleared the snow in the driveway to make way for Ann to get out.

"Such a cold start to your holiday," Charles said. "It must be around 0 °F out there. I certainly hope that you packed plenty of warm clothes."

"Otherwise, I recommend the layer-upon-layer method. That usually works too," Fi said.

"You have such a cool house. I know I must have said it at least ten times yesterday, but I really mean it. I just love this kitchen with the open fireplace and all. It's awesome!" Beate said. "It's almost like camping. Do you ever cook your dinner in the fireplace?"

"Yes, we do, in fact most Indian dishes, like the corn pancakes we had last night, taste better when cooked over an open fire," answered Charles. "We have this old, cast iron frying pan that we use on the embers. And it's both cozy and practical to eat in the kitchen, especially when we have guests."

"So, what are your plans for today?" Charles asked.

"I just have to measure my blood count," said Victoria, "then I would love to go to town. That always seems like a perfect place to start when you visit somewhere new!"

"To town? You mean downtown Pennfield?" Ann laughed from the doorway. "There really isn't much to do here, but you're most welcome to come to Saint John with me."

"That sounds like a wonderful idea. You can ride with Ann, and I can come and pick you up. You just call me. " Charles winked at them. "Young ladies like you must experience town on their own!"

Victoria returned to the bedroom to do her measurements. She pricked herself in the finger with a needle that resembled a pen. She then distributed the small drop of blood that emerged in some tiny holes in an otherwise flat dish. She pushed the dish into a small container. It looked a bit like a very small microwave oven. When she pushed the 'on' button, the inside of the container filled with red light. Later she would be able to read some digits on the display. She had to record these digits in a table.

When she was done, she called home. John answered the phone. He was happy to know that the trip had gone well.

"Your mom is still at work. It might be another couple of hours before she returns," John said, "due to the time difference, you know."

"Time difference? Gosh, I had completely forgotten about that," Victoria laughed. "But okay, just let her know that everything is fine. Beate and I are off to town now."

"I'll let her know. You don't need to spend all your money making phone calls. Just text us, will you?"

"I'll do that. Take care. Give my love to Mom." Victoria hung up and started looking for her warmest clothes. Fi had recommended layers upon layers. Saving time, Victoria simply tipped her suitcase upside down.

* * *

This time around, they enjoyed the beautiful snow-covered landscape along the 40 mile route leading to downtown Saint John.

Earlier that day they had looked up Mary Joan Steward on the Internet. It turned out that she lived in Saint Stephen. According to the map, Saint Stephen was right on the border between Canada and the USA. There was a bus service from Saint John to Saint Stephen, and in Saint John there was a bus stop at a place called Lancaster Mall.

"Could you drop us of at Lancaster Mall?" Victoria asked. "We are planning to start our expedition there."

When Aunt Ann had made the drop, they waved at her as the Range Rover swerved out of the parking lot. As soon as she was out of sight, the girls headed for the bus.

"Fifty-six dollars for two tickets to Saint Stephen. That's robbery!" exclaimed Victoria.

Beate searched the many pockets of her bag. Finally, she found a library card for the university library. Most pupils got one when they started doing research papers at school.

"Don't you have one of these?" Beate asked.

Victoria did. The woman in the ticket booth glanced briefly at their foreign student IDs. Then she reduced the price to 35 dollars.

Victoria tried Mary Joan's phone number. No one was in, but an answering machine picked up the call.

"Hello, my name is Victoria. I'd like to talk to you about your website and the Christmas wing ding. You can reach me at this number…" When she had recited her number, she pressed disconnect and leaned back into her seat. "Maybe we've let ourselves get carried away by all this. We should have called ahead! I hope she's just out shopping. Otherwise, we might have wasted 70 dollars."

"Calm down. If she isn't there, we will make an appointment when she gets back to us. There must be a café in Saint Stephen where we can hang. Anyway, it will probably be easier for your granddad to pick us up in Saint Stephen than Saint John. It looked slightly closer to Pennfield on the map!"

The bus trip lasted almost two hours due to the snow lying everywhere. Saint Stephen was on the coast, and was the last bus stop on the route. In Saint Stephen the road crossed a broad bridge, and continued into the state of Maine, USA.

When they reached their stop, the girls got off

the bus. They were met by a gigantic sign reading: 'Welcome to Saint Stephen, the Chocolate Town of Canada'.

"Hey, the sign says chocolate!" Beate was thrilled. "Things are looking up!"

The town reminded them of a Danish suburb, with its rows of large houses. Only a few of them had more than one floor. They followed the main road, called King Street, toward the harbor. The harbor was lined with shops and restaurants.

"We have to find Albert Street," said Victoria.

On the far side of the street was an info booth. Traffic was light, and they crossed the street with ease. Inside they found a city map. The map indicated that they had to continue along King Street and then turn right on Main. It wasn't more than a quarter of a mile or so.

The constant cold wind blowing in from the bay felt unpleasant, and they were both relieved and excited when, ten minutes later, they found themselves outside Mary Joan's house.

Hopefully she was home.

The house stood out from the neighboring ones. It was bigger, and positioned further away from the street. It was a three-story house made of red brick.

The walls were covered with vines, and therefore appeared more green than red. The driveway could easily fit ten cars. However, now there was only one.

Victoria walked up the steps and knocked on the heavy door. It flew open almost immediately. The woman in the doorway was slim, and probably in her late thirties. She wore a purple dress and moccasins. Her long hair was the color of nougat and her skin fair as vanilla ice cream. She looked at them questioningly.

"Hello, my name is Victoria. I left a message on your answering machine earlier today."

Mary Joan's face lit up in a wide smile.

"I've been waiting for you. Do come in!" Her high-pitched voice was both inviting and kind.

They stepped into the hallway, where the floor was covered with rugs and animal hides.

Sculptures carved in wood decorated the room. A bear sculpture made of darkened oak presided over a corner of the hallway. It was about three feet tall and decorated with feathers and pearls. The bear stood on its hind legs, facing any visitors entering the house, frozen in a roar.

When Victoria walked past the bear, she felt a jab of pain in her right shoulder. The pain shot all the way down her arm. She stopped in shock.

Mary Joan noticed.

"It's very lifelike. Legend has it that, when Big Bear and Little Bear guard your entrance, no intruders can enter. Unfortunately, Big Bear has been lost, but you get the general idea of what you might have been up against when you suddenly stand face-to-face with this Little Bear." She waved them across the living room to a couch in the corner.

Mary Joan's husband was at work, and her three children were all in school.

Beate and Victoria waited on the deep couch while Mary Joan busied herself in the kitchen making tea. On the wall were pictures with various Indian motifs. More carved sculptures filled a large bookcase. The floor was laid with light-colored tiles and in the middle of the room, was a giant chandelier containing at least 50 red and white candles. It had to be a marvelous sight when they were all lit.

"How may I help you?" asked Mary Joan when they were all seated, each with a mug of hot nettle tea.

"Victoria found your website on the Internet, and she…" Beate started, but Victoria interrupted her.

"My family—the Hanssons in Pennfield—

originate from this area. That's why I'd like to learn more about the old cultures and local rituals. As Beate mentioned, we could tell by your website that you know a lot about Indian culture. We also read about the event that you're planning for Christmas. We'd love to participate, if we can."

"The Hanssons in Pennfield, you say? Well, that makes you part of one of the oldest families here," Mary Joan looked at Victoria with glee.

"Yes," Victoria said proudly. "My grandparents are Charles and Fione. Do you know them?"

Mary Joan shook her head. "No, not personally, but I've certainly heard of them. I actually know a whole lot about your family's history. I'm very interested in the old tribes and their legends. Some of their customs are still alive and well today, you know." Mary Joan was talking fast, as if she was afraid the girls would disappear if she paused. "My little Indian association is just one among many. But we have several major events every year. Next week, we're going to build a sweat lodge by the visitors' center. I am very curious to see if we will succeed in heating up the tent in this cold weather."

"The visitors' center? Is that the one at Quoddy Head?"

"Yes, there's a ritual site on the coast, but with no roads to Quoddy Head, and six feet of snow, we're going to have the event at the visitors' center instead. If the highways are safe for traffic, that is. You're more than welcome to join us!"

"What does it mean to build a sweat lodge?" asked Victoria.

"We put up a large tent and heat it up. Just like a sauna. But the point of building a sweat lodge isn't the heat, but the dream visions."

"Dream visions," Beate repeated. "You mean hallucinations?"

"No, absolutely not. Dream visions are an old Indian insight. They occur after a combination of high temperatures and some original Indian brews."

"Indian brews? Do you mean drugs?" Victoria looked startled, but Mary Joan shook her head.

"There are no illegal drugs. It is simply a uniquely blended tea. It's made from berries and is quite harmless, but if you drink it while overheated, then you might experience visions. In the old days, Indians would find the answers to lifes big questions in their sweat lodges."

Beate nodded eagerly, "That sounds really exciting."

"How come you're so into Indian culture? I mean, you're not Indian yourself, are you?" asked Beate.

Mary Joan smiled. "Well, one should not judge a bottle by its label, as they say. I may not have black hair or brown skin, but I am, in fact, part Penobscot. It's a tribe that lived south of the border. Many of the tribal members left the area back in 1777, when the War of Independence ravaged the land. Some went to Europe and found a new home in Central Europe. An area called the Carpathian Mountains. Have you ever heard of them?"

The girls shook their heads in unison.

"The Carpathian Mountains lie in the border area between Slovakia, Ukraine and Romania. A very influential Carpathian family lived there. They claimed to be descendants from the Dracul family that held the Transylvanian throne back in the fourteenth century." Mary Joan cracked a smile. "Yes, most people don't know this, but there really was a character called Dracul once. He inspired Bram Stoker to write his famous novel about Count Dracula. Well, this Carpathian family was obsessed with power, and they had an enormous knowledge about mythological beings and magical objects from around the world. The Penobscot tribe had a very powerful medicine man. Somehow, the Carpathians knew that and, when the tribe arrived, the Carpathians welcomed them warmly. The Penobscots decided to settle down in the Carpathian Mountains, and soon they were included in the Carpathian organization—and part of their quest for supernatural power that would allow them to rule the area. The Carpathians were determined and cynical and, with help from the medicine man, they exploited the locals' natural superstition. With a combination of raw violence and murder, they actually succeeded. They had a kind of monarchy revolving around this ancient crystal throne. They believed that it held magic powers. More tea?" Mary Joan held out the teapot.

"Oh, yes please," Victoria nodded, blinking due to the sudden change in topic. "What happened then?"

"As the years went by, the tribe was divided in two groups. The Carpathians had assimilated the medicine man and his closest friends, and were a contemptuous bunch. However, there were others who no longer wanted to be part of the violence on which the Carpathians based their power, and wanted to leave. In the end there was a huge argument between them all and, as a result, the moderate part of the family returned to the States. That's the part of the family I come from.

"Later, things went very wrong for those who stayed in Europe. The medicine man died, and he had not trained a successor. As a result, the Carpathians lost their position of power. I am well aware that this all sounds like fiction," she said, laughing. "However, it's true nonetheless. Later the Carpathians were scattered all over Europe. But they didn't give up. They had had a taste of power and desperately wanted it back, whatever the cost. They started searching for a new medicine man who could serve their throne. At the beginning of the century, some of them even came to Canada. It was not a pleasant family reunion, as it turned out they wanted to bring our medicine man back to Europe with them. At first, they tried to convince him to go, and when that didn't work, they tried to abduct him. One morning they rushed his house. There was a skirmish, and several of my ancestors were killed, but in the end the medicine man fought them off. To escape, the Carpathians used the medicine man's daughter as a hostage. The medicine man was furious and the Carpathians were chased all the way to the sea where, rumor has it, he set the sky on fire.

Whatever happened, most of the Carpathians were killed and the medicine man's daughter was finally freed. We haven't heard from them since!"

The girls' eyes were big as saucers.

"My great-grandparents were alive then. They told me the story!" Mary Joan said.

"Wow, some story. A feud between a tribe of braves and the clan of an ancient crystal throne!" Beate laughed.

"Are they Romanian? I mean are they gypsies?" asked Victoria.

"No, they're not gypsies. As I mentioned before, the Carpathian Mountains lie between Slovakia, Ukraine and Romania. The Carpathians don't feel they belong to any one of these countries, or any nation when it comes to that. They merely refer to themselves as Carpathians. Their mission is to regain control of their old homelands. They want to create a state of their own, and rule it."

Victoria leaned back into her seat. It sounded a whole lot like the things Sarah had told her about her family. Could Sarah be related to these Carpathians?

Victoria had an uneasy feeling in her stomach.

"If you like, you are welcome to help out with

the preparations for the sweat lodge," said Mary Joan. She looked at them keenly.

Victoria flashed her widest smile. "We'd love to!"

* * *

Mary Joan gave them a lift to the station, where there was a bus departing for Pennfield. The snow had rendered most of the town motionless around them by the time the bus finally came crawling toward them.

Victoria suddenly thought of something, "How about that bear in the hallway?"

Beate nodded. "It was…ew! I don't think the bones and feathers around its neck were plastic."

"When I passed it, I felt a jab of pain in my right shoulder and a tightening in my chest. It was strange. And the pain felt just like that time in Sarah's garden, when I was stung by a bee. How about you? Did you feel anything?"

Beate shook her head.

"Then it was probably nothing…." Victoria went quiet for a moment, while her thoughts soared.

"It's weird. Those Carpathians Mary Joan was talking about…and Sarah and Roberto…I mean, they are really cool and all, but…." Victoria looked thoughtful. "Remember I told you that Sarah was wearing an old fashioned brooch? I thought it was a bit weird because she looked so smart otherwise. It was basically just a pin with a white mother of pearl head. Thinking about it, the brooch did look a bit like gypsy jewelry."

"That's funny," Beate said agitatedly. "And she told you that her family originally came from Romania, and is now scattered across Europe?"

"Just like the Carpathians when they lost their power. First it's the mad doctor and his organization, and then Sarah and her family pop up out of nowhere, and move in on my street. I mean, we don't exactly live in the city. It's certainly a strange coincidence!"

Suddenly, the air in the bus felt cold. Victoria shivered. She found another jumper in her backpack and placed it over her knees, but she couldn't get warm again.

* * *

They got off the bus in Pennfield and half slid, half skated toward the house. Charles and Fi were surprised to see them.

"I thought I was going to pick you up in Saint

John," Charles exclaimed.

"There was no need. It was easy to get here by bus," Victoria quickly said.

"So, did you find something exciting to do?" Charles asked while they hung their coats in the wardrobe.

"Yeah, we had a good time," Victoria said.

"Ann said she dropped you of at the mall. Did you find something interesting in there?" Charles asked.

"No, not really!" Victoria said looking away.

Charles looked suspiciously at the girls. "You DIDN'T find anything interesting in a mall?"

Victoria felt his gaze. He was examining her face. She looked down.

"Already getting yourselves into trouble, are you?" Charles said.

Victoria blushed as she looked up, but then she saw his smile.

"All right, spill it!" he said.

"Actually we took a small trip down the coast and ended up in Saint Stephen," Victoria confessed.

"Saint Stephen? That was an odd place to visit. I would have thought two young ladies like you would have preferred to traipse all over Saint John," Fi declared as she appeared from the kitchen holding an appetizing pan of stew—which she had quickly whipped up when the girls suddenly returned.

Victoria looked directly at Beate for help, but she had her poker face on.

Victoria breathed in deeply. Why was it so hard to tell the truth?

They were her grandparents, and if anyone would understand the need for an Indian angle on all of this, it would be them!

"On the Internet we read about this local historian with Indian roots, who lives in Saint Stephen," Victoria explained. "She runs a small Indian society. She's a descendant of the Penobscot tribe and she told us some interesting stuff about the region's history. Maybe you've heard of her? Her name's Mary Joan Steward." Victoria broke off a big piece of cornbread and dipped it in the remaining stew on her plate.

"A descendant of the Penobscot tribe! We've heard of her alright, but have never met her," Charles said.

"Was she able to answer some of your questions, then?" Fi asked.

Victoria looked at the two old Indians and was overwhelmed by guilt. She shouldn't have kept this from them at all. What was she thinking?

They were her grandparents!

Besides, if anyone knew anything worth knowing about Indian legends, surely it would be them.

"Mary Joan told us about her family, and she really knows a lot about the local Indian myths. It was all very exciting," Victoria said.

Fi nodded.

Victoria took a deep breath. "And we also wanted to ask her about the thunderbirds!"

"What about the thunderbirds?" Fi asked.

"We've done a lot of reading on thunderbirds. In the myths it was a special potion that provided the thunderbirds with their great powers. We'd like to know more about this potion and how it's made. It might help me deal with my illness!" Victoria held her breath.

Charles wrinkled his brow. "What makes you think that an old Indian potion might offer relief for osteoporosis?"

Victoria swallowed hard. "The doctors say it's osteoporosis, but I don't think they have a clue as to what's wrong with me..." She hesitated for a moment, then continued in a soft whisper, "and I think it will work because I've already tried it!"

Fi and Charles stared at her. Then they looked at each other.

"It was a mad doctor at a clinic in Germany who gave it to me. For a while, it made my bones strong. It made ME strong! And, on top of it all, my senses went ballistic. I could hear things from a mile away and I could see the stripes on a bee across the lawn. However, Mom and John don't believe me. They think that it was just my imagination, a kind of trick of the mind. But they're wrong. It worked!"

Fi broke the silence, "If the potion worked for Victoria, it must mean that…" She stopped and looked at Charles.

"What are you saying?" Victoria asked.

Charles sighed. "Naturally, we have considered if your illness meant that you were next in line. But it is just not possible!"

"The next what?" Victoria stared at them.

"Thunderbird!" Fi almost whispered.

Beate interrupted. "Victoria? A bird? Really?"

"BEATE!" Victoria hushed. "Be serious."

"Of course it's not a real bird," Charles said and a little smile crossed his lips.

"A thunderbird is a magical being. But in order for you to understand, we must tell you more about the thunderbirds," Fi said. She took a small ornament off a shelf on the wall behind her. It was a bird of prey carved from a tooth.

Victoria looked at the small figurine. Considering its size, it must have been a big tooth, maybe from a bear?

"To the Abenaki people, and therefore also to the Passamaquoddy tribe, the thunderbirds are believed to be sacred creatures. Legends tell us how the thunderbirds battled against the Bird from the East." Fi held out the small bird ornament. "I know it doesn't look like much," she laughed. "The thunderbirds were men who had relinquished their human bodies. Instead, they turned into demigods of a sort. In the legends, all the bones in their bodies being crushed illustrated this transition. Afterward, the men were resurrected in the spirit of the thunderbird. However, not everyone could be a thunderbird. Only those who have, what science today would call, the proper gene can be reborn as a thunderbird. The gene only appears in the Abenaki people." Fi straightened up with a smile. "In fact, most of the thunderbirds have been found in our small line of the Abenaki people, the Passamaquoddy tribe. Those who had the gene were quite frail, but at the same time, they were the only ones who could become thunderbirds. Back in the day, we said they were 'marked by the thunderbird', but today we call them carriers of the glass, or crystal, gene because they break at the slightest strain."

"So you have to have the crystal gene to become a thunderbird," exclaimed Beate.

"And then the potion only works if you have it!" Victoria seconded.

"Yes. Exactly," said Fi.

"But does the body really need to be crushed into a pulp in order for the person to become a thunderbird?" asked Victoria.

"We don't know what happens in the ritual when a person is welcomed into the ranks of the thunderbirds. I don't think that the crushing should be taken too literally though. The way I see it, the bodies of those who have the crystal genes are already crushed repeatedly—every time they break a bone. Like you, Victoria. Can you even remember how many times you broke your leg or your arm?" Charles asked.

Victoria tried to remember, but she gave up. "I don't know the exact number. Maybe 30 times. Give or take."

"You see my point?" Charles said.

Both girls nodded.

Victoria felt relieved.

"And, when the person takes the potion..." Victoria started.

"He gets strong, very strong. All his senses are reinforced and his bones become unbreakable." Charles finished her sentence.

"You keep saying 'he' and 'him', but doesn't the potion work on women?" Beate asked.

"No, only men can get the crystal gene, and it only works if you have it. Otherwise there is no effect at all," Charles said.

"You are an odd case! What you're telling us is impossible. But if the potion the doctor in Germany gave you had the effect that you described, it must be because you have the crystal gene," said Fi. "And I'm still having a hard time believing it!"

"But there is more to it," Charles continued. "In order to become a thunderbird, there is a ritual, a sort of test the person has to pass. If he passes the test, he transforms into a thunderbird. That means that he is given the necessary insight and special powers to fight evil."

"By insight, you mean that he...SHE also learns how to produce the potion that I tested?" Victoria interrupted, almost out of breath.

"Yes, among other things. But the gene isn't an easy gift to pass on. If the heir doesn't pass the test, he can't make the potion and then he must live a lifetime with brittle bones. And the test itself is certainly not without danger! Many of those who have tried have died in the process. And here's the thing," Charles said, "your dad had the crystal gene!"

"Wow, this is crazy!" Beate said.

"Yes, you're right. In our modern world where no one believes in anything and everything must be explained scientifically, it is crazy," Charles agreed.

"As you perhaps have figured out by now, the hunting trip during which your dad disappeared was no ordinary hunting trip," Fi revealed.

Victoria felt her blood pulsating hard in her temples. "Then what really happened to him?"

Charles threw his arms in the air.

"That's exactly it! We don't know. Normally, they find the bodies of those who don't pass the test, but your dad just disappeared. Of course we couldn't tell the police the truth, so we told them that he was out hunting when he went missing."

"And what about my mother?"

"Your dad never told her about the thunderbirds.

He was afraid that she would think he was crazy. And she probably would have! But we know that he intended to tell her when he got his powers," said Charles.

"So we had to tell your mother the same story that we told the police," Fi added.

"So this hunting trip was a sort of quest to pass a test? Do you know what he had to do?"

Charles shook his head.

"We don't really know that much. Your dad didn't even know what to expect. Of course, the tribal elders, and our medicine man Bill Backsteps, tried to guide him. But Bill is not a thunderbird, and he only knows what has been passed on to him from his predecessors."

"But it all fits!" Victoria said. "If my dad had the crystal gene, and I have this disease, then why didn't someone figure out that I also have the crystal gene? Who even says that a thunderbird gets a boy who can inherit the gene? Half the time parents get girls! It's really discriminatory and not at all logical if you think about it."

"If we had known, we could have helped. We would have helped! But the gene has always been passed from man to man. The gift has NEVER been passed down to a woman," Fi said, emphasizing the word 'never'.

"And furthermore, the crystal gene isn't passed on from parent to child. It normally skips a generation or two. It jumped from your great-granddad to your dad," said Charles.

"We saw the signs, but just didn't think it was a possibility. And when your father disappeared and we lost contact, we had to let it go. It was strange, yes, but nevertheless, it had to be an unfortunate coincidence!" Fi put her hand on Victoria's arm.

"Charles and I will summon the tribal elders for a pow wow. We need to talk this over," said Fi.

"A pow wow is a meeting where we debate things that concern the tribe. Almost like a board meeting. We pile all our knowledge together and decide how to deal with important matters," Charles explained.

"It will be totally cool meeting all the old timers!" said Beate.

"A pow wow also means a meeting for the tribal elders *only*," Charles continued.

Beate looked disappointed.

"By the way," Victoria said. "Mary Joan is planning to build a sweat lodge next week. It's the first time they have tried making one in the winter.

She has done a lot of research about the Abenaki tribes and their ceremonies. Maybe she knows something. Can we go?"

"Of course, you can," Fi said. "It sounds like fun."

Chapter 8
Mary Joan's Christmas Wing Ding

Pennfield, 16 December 2017

Dear Diary,

My life has taken a bizarre turn.

A couple of months ago, the doctors thought that I suffered from an incurable disease. Now it turns out I might not even be sick. Instead, I belong to an ancient line of people, and I'm 'the chosen one'.

And my dad was too!

It's out of this world☺☺☺.

Today, Beate and I helped Mary Joan Steward build a sweat lodge. She's a local historian who knows everything worth knowing about Indian legends. The day after tomorrow, we're going to participate in an event in the sweat lodge. Mary Joan calls it a wing ding. It's mostly for fun because wing ding means party. And we're going to be sweating. You can hardly call that a party☺.

And there are more exciting things to follow!

Grandma and Grandpa have called a pow wow!

It will be on 20 December. Formally, you have to call a pow wow months in advance, but this time the elders have agreed to come on short notice. Probably because of the urgency of what they have to debate (meaning me)☺.

I haven't broken any bones in months. Actually, I've been in tip-top shape since I had the potion. In fact, everything is going very well right now and, for once, being me is awesome☺.

It was early morning on 18 December. Beate and Victoria were cold. They stood outside in the driveway, waiting for Charles to bring the pickup around. He had promised to take them to Saint Stephen. From there, they would catch a ride with Mary Joan to the visitors' center at Quoddy Head, where they were going to have the Christmas wing ding.

From Mary Joan's house they had to drive approximately 50 miles and the weather had not improved. Snow fell heavily on the roads, and all that was navigable was a narrow track that the plows had managed to clear.

It took almost two hours before Mary Joan's Range Rover plowed its way into the parking lot at the visitors' center. Another car was already there.

"That will be Peter Two Hawks," Mary Joan said when she saw the car. "I do hope he brought his sons with him. Jeremy and Storm are such helpful boys."

Victoria threw open the car door and climbed out of her warm seat. She breathed in deeply. She felt the icy air crystalizing in her throat. She shivered and pulled her scarf up so it covered her mouth and nose. She would never get used to this cold.

They made their way through the thick snow to the entrance of the visitors' center. Halfway there, they heard the sound of bells behind them. It was a snowplow, drawn by two horses. In the seat sat two people wrapped in heavy coats.

"Mary Joan! How wonderful it is to see you!" Deep, dark eyes above a white, gleaming smile greeted them. Peter Two Hawks jumped off the sledge and gave Mary Joan a hearty hug.

"This has turned out to be quite a success. I'm expecting 22 visitors, some of them from as far away as Florida and British Columbia," Mary

Joan explained, rubbing her hands in delight.

"That sounds good," Peter said. "Jeremy and I will clear the road as far as Saint Lubeck so people can get in."

Back on the sledge, the second passenger pulled his hood back and smiled at them. Jeremy Two Hawks was 19 years old, with light brown skin, short dark hair, high cheekbones and perfect white teeth.

"Wow!" Victoria said aloud without thinking. Beate immediately elbowed her in the ribs. "That was my line," she whispered in Danish.

"Now the snow has stopped, it actually looks like it's going to be a nice, clear day," Peter Two Hawks said. "Storm is inside. If you bring the groceries to the kitchen, the three of you can prepare the lunch." He nodded toward the boxes of food in the back of Mary Joan's Range Rover. "We'll be back in an hour or so. Probably just in time for the first guests to arrive." He swung back into his seat. He turned the sledge around and disappeared back down the road.

Each carrying a box, they stepped directly into the large common room of the visitors' center.

At the far end was Storm, the younger of Peter Two Hawks' sons. Storm had the fire going in an enormous open fireplace—it was made with huge boulders and took up most of the far wall.

"Hello there, Mrs Steward," Storm called out across the room when he noticed them. "Why don't I give you a hand with those boxes?" He grabbed the box Beate was carrying and went through a door into the kitchen.

As soon as the door closed behind him, Beate pinched Victoria's arm.

"What do they feed them in that family? Give him a couple of years, and he'll be as deadly as his brother!"

"We simply have to get a photo of those two guys. Otherwise no one will believe us when we get back home," Victoria giggled.

"Duh," Beate said, hitting her forehead with the heel of her palm. She dug into her pocket for her phone. Phone in hand, she purposefully headed for the kitchen. Victoria, still holding a box, followed her with a smile.

In the kitchen, small frames with Indian

pencil drawings covered the walls.

Most of the drawings showed scenes from Indian ceremonies.

"Oh look," Beate cried, and snapped photos with the camera on her phone. Then she turned to Storm. "Smile!" she demanded—and took his picture.

Even though Storm was only 15 years old, he knew his way around the kitchen. He spoke perfect English, but with a distinctly French accent. He showed the girls where to put the groceries and then they emptied the car of the rest of Mary Joan's stuff.

Afterward, Storm told them what to do in order to prepare the food, and they all helped. When Peter and Jeremy returned at 11:45, lunch was ready and the table in the common room was set.

The door swung open again revealing a man and a woman.

"Mr and Mrs Adams, welcome!" Mary Joan called out from the doorway leading to the common room. "Please come have a seat."

During the next hour, most of the guests

arrived. Everyone was happy and excited, chatting and laughing loudly.

Victoria was sitting next to Jeremy. He was talking to the man on his right. His voice was strong and he spoke in the same French accent as Storm.

"So you decided to spend Christmas with a group of nutheads raising tents in the middle of winter?"

Victoria almost choked on her sandwich when Jeremy spoke to her.

"I just had to come! We hardly have any snow in Denmark, and winter camping is just not the same without it!"

He laughed and the pleasant, ringing sound allowed Victoria to compliment herself on the snappy remark.

He looked up and down the long table.

"I promised Mary Joan to help out during lunch, I better go fill the jugs with fresh water," Jeremy said. He got up and went to the kitchen.

The door swung open again and a woman entered.

"Hello Mrs Southby," Mary Joan greeted her above the noise. "It's lovely of you to join us once again."

Mrs Southby was a beautiful woman in her mid-thirties. Her long black hair was held back in a tight ponytail, and her dark brows were the shape of butterfly wings. She wore a fur vest over a tight, lacy blouse, and a mini skirt. When she noticed everyone's eyes were on her, her face lit up.

"Oh, call me Diane," she said in a bubbly voice. She glanced around the room and spotted Storm, who was talking to Beate.

"Hello Storm," she said as she approached them.

"Good evening, Mrs Southby," he answered.

Beate noticed that the woman wore an old fashioned hairpin. The pinhead was red. It looked completely out of place on the otherwise modern and sharply dressed woman.

Diane Southby took a long look at Beate. Then she turned and looked around. She spotted the empty seat next to Victoria, where

Jeremy's plate was set.

"Maybe there's a space for me right there?"

Victoria noticed Jeremy returning from the kitchen with jugs of fresh water.

She gestured at him but before she could say anything, Diane pulled the chair out from the table and sat down.

"I haven't seen you around before. Must be your first time attending. Tell me, how do you fit into this whole hullabaloo?" Diane asked Victoria while she got herself settled. She crossed one leg over the other and, in doing so, her skirt crept up and revealed most of her leg. Her voice was still bubbly, but her tone hinted that she was used to people listening when she spoke—and that they complied when she raised her voice.

"Oh...I'm distantly related...to..." Victoria said, looking around at the people at the table, "...to Jeremy. He is my...cousin!" Victoria held on tightly to her chair. What had possessed her to lie?

"Oh, so you're a Two Hawks," Diane

concluded.

Victoria swallowed hard.

Jeremy's cousin!

That would be hard to explain later.

Suddenly she felt a prickly, buzzing sensation in her shoulder.

"What about yourself? Why are you here?" Victoria thought her voice sounded distant.

Diane's smile seemed to fade for a brief second. It was as if Victoria had hit a nerve. "*I* am also related to *them*."

Victoria did not care for the way she said 'them'.

"I hear you're visiting from Denmark. How much family lives there, I wonder?" Diane said pushing for more information.

Victoria squirmed.

How could Diane know about her? Who had she been talking to?

And why?

If Diane knew who she was, then she probably also knew that she wasn't related to the Two Hawks family.

And that she had lied!

She needed to collect her thoughts. She had to get away from Diane. She tried to make eye contact with Beate, but Beate did not see her. She was chatting with Storm and, judging by her loud giggles, they were having a good time.

Just then, a voice interrupted Victoria's thoughts of escape.

"Come cousin, it is time to light the fire in the sweat lodge!"

Before Victoria could excuse herself, Jeremy pulled her off her seat. He led her in the direction of the back door and out onto the small lawn where the sweat lodge had been built.

Victoria's cheeks had turned deep red. "...Us being related, I can explain," she began, as soon as the door closed behind them.

"Don't worry about it," Jeremy interrupted her. "I've met her a couple of times and I don't care much for her either. I can't really put my finger on it. There's just something about her that makes you want to keep personal things to yourself. She's nosey—a busybody!"

"I think she is kind of witch-like," Victoria

replied.

Jeremy nodded. "Yes, that too!"

They walked to the sweat lodge along a narrow pathway that Jeremy and his dad had cleared in the snow.

"I'm just so excited about this," Victoria said, disturbing the silence. "I hope there will be dream visions tonight. On film you always get to meet your totem spirit…." Victoria stopped. She was babbling like a crazy woman! "Maybe I should go and find my coat," she said frantically—she wanted to get back to the common room.

Where was Beate when you *really* needed her?

Jeremy smiled. In fact, he did that a lot. And it made him look even hotter!

"We're going to start a fire in a sweat lodge. Do you really think you need your coat?"

Her cheeks reddened again. 'A human version of Rudolph the Red-Nosed Reindeer,' she thought to herself. Then Jeremy began laughing and she couldn't help but laugh too.

It was as if they had known each other for a

long time.

The entrance to the sweat lodge was very low and she had to kneel to get in. A hide served for the tent door, and Jeremy held it aside for her while she entered. The tent was shaped like a dome.

It was spacious enough for 20 people to sit in a circle around the fire. The fireplace itself consisted of a rectangular pile of rocks. Under the rocks was a hole full of firewood.

Jeremy rolled away the stones covering the hole. A fat wick poked through the firewood and ran along the entire length of the fireplace. He flipped open a lighter and lit the wick. With a distant look in his eyes, he watched the wick burn, until the flames reached the firewood. Then he rolled the rocks back into place.

Jeremy sat down and leaned against one of the low backrests. They were simply some wide wooden boards that had been stuck into the ground. Victoria sat down next to him. "I believe you when you say that it's going to be burning hot in here," she said, stressing the 'going to be'. "But right now, I could use a coat!"

He blinked.

"Let's see if we can do something about that."

Victoria swallowed hard. Was he serious or just making fun of her? She had never had a boyfriend before. The mere thought of being warmed by Jeremy made her heart race like a runaway horse. Could he tell? While she desperately searched for something clever to say, he put his arm around her and continued talking.

"Although I also think that Diane Southby is a bit...what did you call it...witch-like?" he started, "*I* am also curious to know the answer to her question. How do you and your friend fit into all of this?"

Again, Victoria swallowed hard. Jeremy sounded like an okay guy, but, ultimately, she didn't really know him. She didn't know if he could be trusted. And it was very hard to think coherent thoughts while sitting there with his arm around her. So close that she could smell his light perfume.

"My dad was from around here. He moved to Denmark when he married my mom. Beate and I are visiting my grandparents in Pennfield. Since we're here, we thought it would be fun to try a sweat lodge."

"Pennfield?" His eyes lit up. "Do you mean the Hanssons?"

"Yes, do you know them?"

Jeremy nodded eagerly.

"Most of the Indians in this area know each other. And the ones you don't know personally, you know by reputation. But I know the Hanssons. Pretty well, actually. They're friends of my dad's, and we've visited them often."

"I was very young the last time I was here," Victoria said. "But I've wanted to visit them for years. Everyone here is just so friendly. I am so happy that I finally made it back!"

"It's funny!" Jeremy said. "I've been to Copenhagen!"

"Really? Awesome. I mean…why?"

"It was the COP 15, back in 2009. CPAWS was sending a delegation and my father was planning to go. I really wanted to go along. At first, my parents said no, because I was only 11.

However, I begged for months, until they finally gave in. I drove them crazy, I think!"

"The oldest trick in the book," Victoria laughed. "Who is CPAWS, by the way?"

"The Canadian Parks and Wilderness Society. It is an environmental association. I still remember that the COP ended in a huge demonstration! More than one hundred thousand people walked from your parliament building—how do you say it? Qristensborg?"

Victoria tried not to smile. Due to his accent, it sounded different when he said it. It sounded both cute and exotic. She nodded, "Christiansborg."

"…All the way to the Bella Center," Jeremy continued, "where the conference was held. The line of people was more than a mile long!"

"I remember seeing it on TV. Did you seriously go all the way to Copenhagen for that?" As soon as she had said it, she wanted to take it back. It sounded all wrong. She didn't mean it like that. Of course environmental issues were important!

He raised an eyebrow. "If nothing is done to

reduce pollution, CO_2 will continue to make temperatures rise. It's changing the world as we know it. In some places, melted ice is causing water levels to rise to such an extent that low-lying countries are experiencing flooding. And there'll be more natural disasters. Phenomena such as El Niño will occur more frequently— droughts, cyclones and tsunamis. Animals disappearing from their natural habitats already affects the livelihood of indigenous people and eventually everyone will suffer. Soon it will be too late to stop it. In fact, perhaps it's already too late!"

"What I meant…I mean, what I was trying to say…" Victoria said. How was she supposed to think straight, sitting that close to him? "It's just that I got the impression that the conference was a failure?" The ground was still cold to sit on and she pulled her legs up in front of her. "But it was very impressive that so many people marched to express their concern." She gazed upward while she silently repeated to herself: 'Think first, then speak!'

Why was that so hard to remember, just because she was sitting next to a good-looking guy?

"I wouldn't call it a complete *failure*.... But let's not talk about that anymore." He tightened his grip around her shoulders.

They sat in silence for a moment. Victoria thought that, somehow, it was a nice kind of silence.

Then he pulled away. He stood up and went to the fireplace to examine the flames raging beneath the rocks.

"The fire looks good. I think the others will be here soon. We better find ourselves a good seat." He unbuttoned his shirt. Victoria watched him take off both his shirt and his tank top. His muscular upper body was a golden brown, just like his face.

"You might want to get undressed, before it gets too hot," he said.

Get undressed?

"Take off my clothes?" Victoria jumped up. She had not seen that coming.

"You're going to sit fully dressed in a sweat

lodge?" he said. Victoria could see that he thought it was amusing.

"I hadn't really given it much thought," she stuttered. "I think I better go...eh...find Beate. She's probably wondering where I am."

At that moment, the hide was lifted aside and Mary Joan entered, closely followed by two other female guests. They were dressed in nothing but small loincloths and had narrow pieces of fabric tied around their chests.

"Oh, there you are, Victoria," she said. "Beate is looking for you."

Victoria mumbled an excuse and pushed her way past Mary Joan. Out of the sweat lodge, she ran across the lawn. When she opened the door to the common room, more guests came through on their way to the sweat lodge. They had all gotten undressed.

"Where have you been?" shouted Beate when she spotted Victoria at the door. "They want us to take off all our clothes and wear these..." For once, Beate lacked a smart remark. "Look at this top. There isn't even enough fabric for a bandana!"

As they finished undressing, the rest of the guests left for the sweat lodge.

Just then, Diane Southby put her hand on Victoria's shoulder. She had also changed into the minimalistic sweat lodge outfit.

"I doubt you will find the answers you're looking for out there," Diane said, gesturing in the direction of the sweat lodge.

Talking to Diane, the stabbing pain in Victoria's shoulder returned. "I'm not even sure I know the questions yet, so how…?"

"Listen, I know what happened in Dresden," Diane continued. "We have everything you need. We have been waiting for someone like you for more than a hundred years!"

"Dresden?" Victoria stammered.

The mad doctor?

How could Diane know about that?

"I have no idea what you're talking about," she said. Her words sounded hollow and distant. She felt her chest tightening as the pain in her shoulder spread to her arm and upper body.

Diane's eyes narrowed. For a second, it looked as if she was ready to shake the truth out of Victoria. Then she controlled herself. "So that's the way you want to play it," she said. It sounded as if she was talking to a small child. She shook her head. "This is a waste of my time. Go to the sweat lodge. You might even lose a few pounds! Maybe afterward you'll realize that you need someone who can help you. Mary Joan and her stupid friends cannot. They are a bunch of fools, I assure you." She sneered audibly, "We on the other hand, can tell you everything you need to know!" She hesitated for a moment. Then she played her trump card, "Who do you think made the potion that Dr Schwartz gave you? We did!"

Victoria heard Diane's words resonate in her head.

Whoever they were, they knew how to make the potion!

They could give her the recipe. She just had to listen to Diane for a few minutes. Then Victoria remembered Dr Schwartz. The fanatical look in his eyes. She recalled how he had pushed her into the wall. *They* were dangerous people!

She lowered her voice. "As I said before. I have no idea what you're talking about. You must have me confused with someone else!"

"All right!" Diane said. "But you must decide today!"

"Decide what?" said Beate, who had been busy putting the minimalistic outfit back in its box.

"It's nothing," Diane said.

Just then Jeremy peered through the doorway. He was wearing a loincloth. "Victoria?" he said. "We're ready to start."

Beate quickly elbowed Victoria in the ribs while keeping her eyes on Jeremy.

Diane looked from one to the other through narrow eyes while fiddling with the pin holding back her hair.

"What's wrong with you people?" Diane sneered. "You should have listened!" She pushed Victoria over and, like a snake, she jabbed at her shoulder. But this time Victoria saw the needle, and managed to push Diane's arm away.

"What the hell?" Jeremy shouted. He rushed across the room and right into Beate, who had thrown herself forward in an attempt to catch Victoria when Diane pushed her. The collision knocked Victoria back into Diane's arms, and the second jab buried the needle deep into Victoria's shoulder.

Quickly, Diane turned around, grabbed her clothes, and left the room in long strides.

A black hole of pain exploded inside Victoria, and all the shapes around her melted together like a 3D movie without the glasses. Then everything went dark.

Jeremy just managed to catch Victoria as her body gave way.

"Stop her!" shouted Beate pointing at Diane. Then she realized that they were alone in the common room. Everyone but them had gone to the sweat lodge.

"Help me," Jeremy moaned. "She needs to lie down!" Beate grabbed a cushion from one of the benches and placed it under Victoria's head. Victoria's face was white as snow, and her breathing was troubled. Jeremy pulled the needle from Victoria's shoulder.

"Go get my dad!"

Beate ran to the sweat lodge and called to Peter Two Hawks to come quickly. He immediately read her face and asked no questions. On the way out of the tent, he gestured to Mary Joan to come too.

"I don't know exactly what happened, but Victoria was stabbed with a huge pin," Beate told the others while they ran back to the common room. "It was that woman, Diane."

In the common room Victoria was lying on the floor. She was unconscious, but breathing.

"Oh my God, Mary Joan yelled, when she saw Victoria, "We must call an ambulance!"

"Let me see the needle," Peter asked, and Jeremy mechanically handed it to his father, who examined it carefully. Then he shook his head. "It's no use calling for an ambulance. The doctors can't help us with this. We must take her to Charles and Fi."

Chapter 9
The Shaman's Needle

THEY QUICKLY WRAPPED Victoria in blankets and carried her to the back seat of Peter's car. Jeremy ran to the sweat lodge to get Storm. While they waited for Jeremy, Mary Joan and Peter got dressed and Beate told them what had happened.

"We need you to stay here and take care of the guests," Peter said when Storm arrived. "Can you do that?"

Storm nodded confidently. "Of course. No problem!"

"Thank you, Storm," Mary Joan said. "Mr and Mrs Adams will help you, but call me if you have any questions!" She reached into her pocket for her keys.

"Hopefully Jeremy and I'll be back before the guests have left," Peter said to his son.

Storm nodded again. "Don't worry, I'm on top of it!"

Mary Joan smiled and handed Storm the keys to the visitors' center.

The back seat of Peter Two Hawks' car was wide and Beate managed to squeeze herself in next to Victoria. She had brought the cushion from the common room, and placed it in her lap for Victoria's head to rest on.

"Let's go!" said Jeremy. He had quickly returned to the common room to dress, and now he climbed into the back seat of the car, opposite Beate. He lifted Victoria's legs onto his lap, to help Beate hold her if the ride should get too bumpy.

Mary Joan got in the front passenger seat, and when she closed the door, Peter turned the ignition and put his foot down. Every time the car jumped and swayed in the snow, Beate and Jeremy did their best to keep Victoria steady in the back seat.

"Did anyone see where Diane ran off to?" Peter asked.

"No, but her car was gone," said Jeremy. Then he smiled to himself. "It must be a cold ride. She was practically naked!"

Mary Joan called ahead to Charles and Fi, who were waiting at the door when they entered the driveway.

"I called Bill Backsteps," Charles said. "He's on his way. He was getting ready for the pow wow but he left immediately when I told him what had happened. It's a long drive to get here, so I don't think he'll make it before morning."

"The sooner the better," Peter said.

"Listen Dad, there's no need for both of us to go get Storm. Maybe you should stay here, Bill Backsteps might need your help." Jeremy said.

"You're right. Just tell your mother what happened, she'll understand."

They watched the tail lights disappear as Jeremy drove off. Then Fi got them all seated in the kitchen. She had made hot cocoa, which she now poured generously into big mugs.

Peter had placed Diane's needle on the table. The shiny surface reflected the golden flames from the fireplace.

"Why is the mother of pearl pinhead white? How is that possible?" Beate exclaimed.

"I don't follow, what do you mean?" Mary Joan said.

"When that woman…Diane…came to the visitors' center I noticed the hairpin. The pinhead was definitely red—now it's white!" Beate explained.

"Are you sure it was red?" Charles asked her.

"Yes, it was dark red."

Charles picked up the needle and studied it closely.

"Why don't we try to wake her up?" said Beate.

"I am afraid we can't. There's not much we can do for her on our own," said Fi.

"What do you mean? There must be something!"

"I know it's hard to just sit here, doing nothing, but we must wait for Bill Backsteps. He's the only one who can save Victoria now," Fi said.

Beate stared at her in disbelief. Her hands trembled and she got cocoa all over the table. Fi put her arm around her.

Mary Joan pointed to the needle. "I realize that there is more to Victoria's condition than just getting pricked by that, but I agree with Beate. There must be something we can do."

"Looks can be deceiving," replied Fi. "Unfortunately, this is one of the notorious shamans' sacrificial needles and, compared to the damage it can inflict on Victoria's soul, the prick itself is nothing more than a scratch."

Mary Joan looked shocked. "I've read about the shamans' needles, but I never thought they were real!"

"Why is it called a sacrificial needle? What happens now?" Beate asked. She was pale as snow.

"The needle has branded Victoria. When a human is branded, evil creatures from the spirit world can catch her scent and attack her," Charles explained.

"Catch her scent and attack her?" Beate swallowed hard. Her voice shrieked, "Can't we throw the evil spirits off her trail somehow? Use garlic or something?"

"No, it is not that simple. At first, the shaman draw a little blood from the victim, to tempt a spirit and give it the person's scent. Like when a bloodhound smells the clothes of the person it has to track down. If you know what to look for, you can usually tell when a shaman is up to no good. The first time the victim is pricked, the pinhead changes from white to blood red. Then the needle is loaded with the victim's blood and the spirits can taste the blood from the needle. A bit like bait on a fishhook. Eventually, one of them will take the bait. The best shamans may even be able to choose which spirit they want for the assignment. That way they build relationships based on dependency—blood ties—with selected spirits."

"About a month ago, there was an incident. Victoria was talking to this girl, Sarah, who had just moved in next door. Out of the blue, she felt a pain in her shoulder, she thought she had been stung by an insect. Victoria mentioned that Sarah was wearing an old-fashioned brooch—white mother of pearl. It was a weird piece of jewelry for a young girl to wear. What if the pin in that brooch was one of those...things?!" Beate gestured toward the needle on the table, "And what if Sarah pricked Victoria with it?" Beate went quiet.

"We can't know that for sure," Charles said.

"But it is a possibility we have to deal with," said Fi.

"Creepy!" said Beate. "But if it is the same pin, and Sarah pricked Victoria with it, then why is the pinhead still white?"

"When a spirit has tasted the blood and taken the bait, the shaman uses the needle once more, to transfer the blood back into the victim, where the *infected* blood is again mixed with the victim's blood. When the needle is emptied of blood, it turns white again. From then on, the victim is branded and can't do anything but wait for the spirit to arrive. That is, if the person even knows what he or she has coming. Naturally, only few people do. How could they? But as I mentioned before, I don't think anyone has seen a sacrificial needle for centuries," Fi sighed.

"Not until now," Charles added. All the color had left his usually suntanned face.

Beate looked at the needle and its white pinhead.

"So a spirit has locked onto Victoria's scent!" She shuddered.

"How come you know so much about this?" asked Mary Joan. "I've read a lot about shamans' needles, but I've never come across these details."

"The shamans were wizards who had spirits in their employ. We know about them because our tribe once fought an invading group of warriors back in the eighteenth century. It was a shaman leading the group. Fortunately, our tribe's medicine man back then was a thunderbird. In a particularly bloody battle, our thunderbird defeated the shaman. Luckily, they wrote everything down, but it was only for the select few to read the scripts. Bill Backsteps, Peter Two Hawks, Fi and I all read the scripts back in our younger days," Charles explained.

Mary Joan's face lit up in a big smile. "The old scripts, you say? They are so rare! You are indeed privileged if you got a chance to read those documents—to discover their secrets, immerse yourself in the ancient stories!"

"Yes, but unfortunately they were lost in a fire back in the sixties." Charles mimicked smoking a joint.

Mary Joan looked disappointed.

"That way we know what we are dealing with,

but only Bill has the power to save her," Charles continued. "At least I hope he does," he added quietly.

"But what happens now? I still don't understand—we can't do anything to help her?" said Beate.

"Right now we can't do anything but help her rest. The high fever will weaken her body, so she mustn't overheat.... You have all had a very long day, so I'll take the first watch and Charles will take over at three in the morning," Fi decided.

"...And then he'll wake me up at six," Beate interjected.

Fi nodded. "But now you must get some rest."

While the others went to their rooms, Fi sat in the living room where they had made up a bed for Victoria on a mattress. Peter had been assigned a room at the back of the house, with a view of the forest, while Mary Joan slept in a guestroom in the attic.

Fi crouched down next to her granddaughter. Tears ran down her cheeks while she put a wet cloth on Victoria's burning hot forehead.

"I am so afraid, but I promise you that we will do everything in our power to get you through this," she whispered.

* * *

That night, Victoria did not wake up even once. She went from burning hot to icy cold, and back to burning hot, while gasping for air like a fish out of water.

On occasion, she would suddenly sit up and point into a dark corner of the room. Pointing at something that only she could see. In her dreams, it was cold and foggy. Something in the fog had a hold on her left arm. Something with claws. Slowly, she was pulled through the fog and into a vast and unknown darkness. She didn't want to go into the darkness, but the hold on her was too strong. Most of her arm had already disappeared into the thick, wavering fog. She wanted to scream, but neither in her dream, nor in Fi and Charles' living room, did any sound make it past her lips.

At 7:30 in the morning, there was a knock on the door. Beate, who was on watch, ran into the hallway to open it. Outside was the oldest man she had ever seen. His skin was like parchment paper, and his long, braided hair shone like silver.

Bill Backsteps had arrived.

He smiled warmly at Beate and stepped inside. Beate yelled up the stairs for the others to come down. Bill went into the living room. He crouched down next to Victoria. He placed his hand on her forehead and pulled her left arm out from underneath the blankets. His face was motionless while he inspected the arm.

Beate gasped. Victoria's arm was the color of cement. From her elbow to her wrist were long, deep marks. It almost looked as if her arm had been caught in a bear trap and she had tried to pull it out.

Bill said something in Indian. Fi hurried into the kitchen to fetch the needle. He examined it briefly. "No doubt about it—it's a shaman's needle!" he concluded.

He got up and handed the needle back to Fi.

"I need Peter to assist me, and I suggest the rest of you stay back so I don't have to worry about your safety too. I'm really not sure what to expect from this demon!"

Fi, Charles, Mary Joan and Beate did as he suggested. Fi put her arm around Beate. "Bill knows what he's doing," she said.

As they stood there, in a corner of Fi and Charles' living room, it was as if the light suddenly faded and in the middle of the darkness was Victoria's pale, white face.

She looked so vulnerable.

Unconscious to the danger she was in.

"I sure hope you're right," Beate whispered, unsure whether Fi was trying to calm her or herself.

Bill asked Peter to put more firewood on the embers in the fireplace. Then he opened his animal-hide bag and pulled out two leather purses. He opened the bigger of the two. It contained a red powder.

While slowly circling Victoria's mattress he poured the red powder onto the floor. That way the red powder formed a closed circle around her.

"Demons can't cross the line," Fi explained.

Bill opened up the second purse, and Peter handed him a bowl of hot water. He poured a brown powder into the water and whisked it fiercely with two eagle feathers from his belt. He whisked so hard that eventually it turned into froth.

Beate jumped in surprise when Bill let out a loud yell. He swung the feathers toward Victoria and some of the froth sprayed onto her face.

The light in the living room went out and came back on. Peter added more wood to the fire.

Flames flared up and bathed Victoria and the old

Indian in a golden glow.

The fire flickered when Bill began to sing an old Indian hymn. Then he swung the eagle feathers toward Victoria once more. This time the froth sprayed onto her left arm, where it bubbled for a second before it vaporized.

Inside the red circle, a mist started rising from the floor.

Bill raised his voice and swung the feathers repeatedly, covering the dead grey skin on Victoria's arm with brown froth.

Beate gasped.

Inside the mist, a silhouette appeared.

It was the silhouette of a creature with fangs and long arms.

Each arm ended in a claw-like hand.

The beast held onto Victoria's arm. It hissed and lashed out at Bill, but the red powder on the floor created an invisible shield and hindered the attack.

Now that Bill could see the creature, he quickly flung the froth directly at its face. When the froth hit, it made the same sound as when a slab of butter is dropped on a very hot pan.

The beast let out a shrieking whine but it did not let go of Victoria.

Instead, it rolled backward and disappeared, dragging Victoria into the mist.

Bill didn't hesitate, he jumped the line of powder and reached down into the mist. He got a hold on the demon's arm and, like a lumberjack in a tug of war, he started pulling at the demon.

When Peter saw what was going on, he too jumped into the circle and reached down into the mist. He got hold of Victoria and started pulling her up. More mist started filling the red circle and Bill yelled to Charles to ignite the powder.

Charles grabbed a log of burning wood from the fireplace, but just as he was about to drop it onto the line of powder, the demon let go of Victoria and lashed at Bill and Peter. Bill ducked and rolled aside, pulling the demon out of the mist and away from Victoria.

Doing so, he lost his grip on the demon and, with a roar, it turned on Peter—who was now standing with Victoria in his arms. With both hands full, Peter was defenseless against its claws and sharp teeth, but, before it could attack, Charles hit the demon with the burning log. Bill lunged forward, pushing the demon up against the invisible wall where Charles threw the entire bowl of froth at it.

The froth made the demon snarl with pain and leap back into the mist.

Finally, Charles could drop the burning log onto the red powder and close the portal to the spirit world. While the ring flared up, Bill helped Peter carry Victoria out of the circle.

Beate noticed that she did not feel any heat from the red flames as they licked against the empty mattress. Then they hissed and died out.

Chapter 10
Carpathians, the German Chapter

IT WAS SITUATED on the outskirts of a small village. From the outside, it looked like a spa hotel. A beech forest with a tangled network of small pathways running in all directions surrounded it. Along the pathways were benches on which guests could sit and ponder life's big questions.

Beneath the hotel, the place changed character. From the hotel foyer, decorated in soft carpeting and tapestries, a wide staircase and a heavy steel door led to an entirely different world. A world of concrete walls, locked and secretive rooms, and, in the middle—the ceremonial hall.

In the ceremonial hall, the seating was arranged in the shape of a spiral winding toward the lowest point of the hall. This was where the elders sat at a round table, facing the other members of the secret brotherhood. The elders were separated from the spiral like the dot underneath a question mark.

Normally the hall was full, but today only the elders were present when Dr Schwartz stepped into the dimly lit room. A young brother escorted him down towards their table.

The higher the rank, the closer you sat to the elders. Normally, Dr Schwartz sat on the second row from the elders, not quite in the inner circle yet. However, he ranked high enough to have access to confidential documents and the items kept hidden in the underground fortress.

Today, instead of his usual row, the young brother led him to an empty seat at the center table. There, three of the elders were waiting for him. They were wearing hooded robes, showing only their motionless faces.

The man in the middle was the highest ranking of them all.

Grandmaster Würher!

The small tufts of hair sticking out from under his hood were steel grey. The same as the color of his eyes. His power was unlimited and neither morality nor conscience tormented him when he carried out his business.

Dr Schwartz did not know why he had been summoned by the elders, but he was confident that, if he played his cards right, this meeting could be to his benefit. He sat down without hesitation, folded his hands in his lap, lowered his head and waited.

The silence in the big room was intense when

Würher finally raised his voice.

"The International Council of Elders is satisfied with your efforts. Your information has been useful. We have been able to track the girl, from Denmark all the way to New Brunswick, Canada, where she is hiding out. Our agent in Canada made contact with the girl and tried to convince her to work with us. Unfortunately, it did not lead to the kind of dialogue we were hoping for, so she had to turn to plan B," said Würher.

"Plan B?"

"When the girl gets her powers she will become very dangerous, and we can't have her running around if she isn't working for us. Therefore, we had her marked by a shaman's needle, just to be ahead of things if she refused to cooperate."

"You sent her to the Shadowlands? I don't see the point," Dr Schwartz said.

"In time we might find a way to control her powers from the shadows, and, until then, we just wait."

Dr Schwartz felt a tension between his shoulders. "But she will be dead then. The only heir that our brotherhood has encountered in a hundred years. What a waste! Did it work then?"

"We are not sure. The girl has powerful friends.

We have been watching them and they show no signs of having lost a relative. We suspect they must have saved her from our demon. And on top of this, sadly, it also means that she is now aware of our presence."

Dr Schwartz shook his head. He couldn't believe what he was hearing. "How could she escape a demon when she was marked by a shaman's sacrificial needle? The people helping her must really know their stuff! What's next?"

Würher's face lit up and he looked directly at Dr Schwartz. "If we could bring her in alive, maybe you could transfuse her blood into one of our own. Steal her bloodline somehow?"

Dr Schwartz stroked his chin. "It might work!" he said eagerly. "How exiting!"

"We can't get to her while she is with the Indians in Canada, but our new Danish chapter is getting ready. They have been working very hard at winning her confidence. If they succeed in getting her guard down, they will snatch her and send her to your clinic in Dresden. We trust that you are up to the task?"

Dr Schwartz felt his blood racing at the thought. He nodded in consent.

"Meanwhile we are taking measures to weaken

her circle of helpers." The elder went quiet, and one of the others took over.

"Brother Schwartz, your efforts so far have pleased us. You may, therefore, move two seats forward. We have great expectations of you in this matter."

Dr Schwartz was not sure what his assignment was yet. He had waited his entire grown-up life to play an important role. Ever since he passed the official ritual and had been seated at the back of the hall.

He breathed in deeply and nodded. Humbly looking down, he got up. When the young brother returned and gently touched his elbow, he followed him out of the hall.

"How is the chapter in Denmark really doing?" the elder asked. The question was aimed at a person who had been hiding behind a curtain covering the wall.

"As I mentioned earlier, our agents are playing their roles, and we are basically done with the house." The heavy curtain was thrown aside and The Wolf stepped out of his hiding place. "However, some of our brothers have caught the attention of the Danish police. This is very unfortunate. To succeed in getting close to the girl, I need some peace and quiet for the next couple of months!"

"Is the Danish chapter already drawing police

attention?" the elder asked.

"No, it's a funny story. Actually, it's the Irish chapter..." The Wolf said.

The elder sighed. "They are very impatient, our brothers in Ireland. Creative, but impatient! Dare I ask what they have come up with now?"

For a brief moment, a rare smile lit up The Wolf's dark face. "One might say they are poaching. In a country like Denmark, they don't always understand the criminal mindset. To the Irish, it opens up all sorts of opportunities. For instance, our Irish brothers discovered that rural Danish museums have tusks, horns and arctic art on display. Ivory in different shapes and forms, but worth millions! They just bought plane tickets to Copenhagen, grabbed the ivory and were gone before anyone realized what was going on. Easy money, but the timing isn't right. We don't need police attention right now!"

The elder nodded.

"The girl has top priority! I will try to control our Irish brothers. Before you return to Denmark, I have another assignment for you. We must do something about the girl's circle of protectors, and one of the targets is already in place. You must leave for Canada as soon as possible and assist our agent in doing what is necessary!"

The Wolf nodded and left the hall with a slight bow.

Chapter 11
Pow Wow

THEY HAD PUT HER in her bed, tucked in between soft pillows and blankets—but still Victoria's sleep seemed restless. Beate on the other hand, didn't sleep at all. She sat upright in her own bed all night, staring at Victoria. She kept telling herself that the demon was really gone.

Then, finally, at 8:30, Victoria opened her eyes.

"She's awake!" Beate yelled and jumped out of her bed. "She's awake!" Beate leaned toward Victoria and grabbed her hand. "How are you feeling? You have been sick. Very sick! Do you remember anything?"

Victoria shook her head. "No," she whispered. Her voice was weak and rusty. She looked around and realized that she was at her grandparents' house. "How did I get here?"

Mary Joan came bursting through the door, closely followed by Charles and Fi. They all gathered around Victoria.

"Thank heaven, you are awake," Fi said.

Charles put his hand on her forehead. "You still feel a bit warm. Are you feeling any pain?"

"No, I'm just really, really..."

"Thirsty?" Bill Backsteps finished her sentence as he came through the door. He handed her the flask of icy cold water he had brought from the kitchen.

Victoria emptied the flask in a few long gulps.

"Fighting demons always drains your body doesn't it?" he said with a smile.

"What happened?" Victoria asked. She looked with horror at the long scars running down her arm. "The last thing I remember is leaving the sweat lodge, because Jeremy said to undress..."

Listening to Beate's vivid description of Diane stabbing her with the needle and the men battling the spirit, all color left her face. Then, the complex explanation on how the sacrificial needle worked made her head start spinning again. When Beate got to the part about how they suspected that Sarah was involved in the whole affair, Victoria stopped her.

"Let's talk about it later, I can't deal with it right now," Victoria stated. "And I'm hungry. Actually, I have never been as hungry as I am now."

"I'm happy to hear it," Fi said. "It's a result of the trauma your body has been exposed to. I'll go make breakfast right away. In the meantime, you can get dressed."

Fi, Charles and Mary Joan left the girls alone. Victoria's arm had been weakened so much that Beate had to help her get dressed. When they came downstairs, the others were seated at the long table.

"Are you feeling okay? Do you feel any pain?" asked Fi, looking at Victoria with a mix of pain and fear in her eyes. Her hand trembled as it tried to bring her cup of tea to her lips.

"My arm feels like rubber, and I have a burning sensation in my shoulder. But otherwise, I'm fine," said Victoria. She pulled up her sleeve and showed the others the deep claw mark that stretched up her arm.

"It's still grey!" Beate said in surprise.

"I have an old recipe that might help," Fi said, and got up. "I even think I have all the ingredients, so I'll make the ointment straight away."

"The moment I met Diane Southby, I just knew that there was something fishy about her," said Victoria. "I could tell that she was a mean bitch."

"More like a witch!" proclaimed Beate.

Victoria looked thoughtful. "Diane mentioned Dr Schwartz, so they must know each other. Could it be that Diane also comes from that part of the

Penobscot tribe that left for Europe back in the eighteenth century?" They all looked at Mary Joan.

Mary Joan considered it carefully. "You might have a point. In fact, the more I think about it, the more likely it seems. Do you remember I told you that the Carpathians also came to Canada?"

The girls nodded.

"They have been here a few times and we know that, while they were here, they contacted several of the tribes. We don't think they had any success recruiting local Indians for their ranks, so perhaps some of them stayed behind, and still live around here."

"Dr Schwartz must have informed Diane about Victoria," said Fi.

"And, somehow, they traced you here, all the way from Denmark. If it was Sarah it all makes sense," Beate sneered. "Who knows what they might do next? They have sacrificial needles, spirits, and probably all sorts of other creepy stuff."

"No doubt they'll try again," said Mary Joan.

Outside the window, dark clouds started rolling in and, within minutes, the bright morning had turned dark.

"I don't understand why someone out there

wants to hurt me," Victoria said as she watched the first raindrops fall from the dark skies.

"Hurt you? They tried to murder you!" Beate said. "If Bill hadn't come, they might have succeeded too. How do you defend yourself against something you can't see...or even understand?"

"We must prepare for the worst," said Charles. He grabbed Victoria's hand. "You are not alone. We'll do everything in our power to keep you safe!"

Everyone looked at Victoria and an impenetrable silence followed.

* * *

The weather stayed dark and it rained all day, and then the elders came. They started arriving next morning. There were ten of them and at lunchtime, everyone gathered in the living room, where a lively fire in the fireplace brightened up the otherwise dark room.

Normally, no one but the elders could participate in the pow wow. But this time nothing was normal. And since it was all about Victoria, the two girls were allowed to sit in.

Charles welcomed everyone in English and reminded them that everything discussed at a pow wow is confidential. Then he told the elders about Victoria having the crystal gene, and the grim attack from Diane.

An older woman tapped Victoria's shoulder. Looking at her intensely she kept repeating something that sounded like '*wisaweyu nipawset macehe*'. Victoria tried to remember to ask Charles for a translation later.

Fi made pancakes with a spicy filling, and when they had finished eating, Charles brought in clay jugs of strong alcohol. Bill Backsteps stood with his back to the fire and his arms folded across his chest, and when everyone had had a drink, they formed a circle around him.

Victoria and Beate also joined the circle. Then, one of the women started making a faint, humming noise. It sounded as if it originated from deep down in her throat. The low vibrating sound increased in strength as more people joined in. In the end, it was as if the air itself vibrated—and, inside the circle, the humming sound felt almost physical enough to lift Victoria right up into the air, if she just let it. With a small nod, Bill opened his arms and the living room went dead quiet.

Even though Victoria knew that the elders and

Beate were standing right next to her, she suddenly felt as if she was alone in a dark, soundless void. She felt panicky, but then there was a hand on her shoulder.

It was Fi.

She pulled Victoria into the middle of the circle, where Bill was now sitting with his legs crossed. His silhouette stood out against the roaring fire and shadows danced around his face. Fi nudged her to her knees, and Bill reached out and held her head in his hands. He began singing in a deep voice. At first, Victoria did not understand any of it. Then the words started shaping images in her head.

She flew across a forest all covered in snow. Somewhere behind her, the sun was rising. Then the forest disappeared underneath her and she shot across the sea, and soared higher and higher into the air. Finally, she slowed down. For a moment, she was suspended in mid-air.

Then the descent started.

She fell faster and faster.

The high speed ripped off her clothes, but she wasn't naked. Instead, she was covered in black feathers. Her arms almost resembled wings. She flapped her arms to reduce her speed as she rushed toward the ground, but it had little effect.

All of a sudden, she noticed a rock formation below her. It looked like the giant head of an Indian. The high speed made the general surroundings seem blurry, but the Indian head somehow stayed in focus. Just as she thought she was going to be smashed to a pulp against its hard surface, the Indian opened his stone eyes and his mouth turned into a dark gap, sucking her in.

Then everything went black.

* * *

"Victoria! How many fingers do you see?"

Victoria was on the couch in Charles and Fi's living room. Her head was pounding and her mouth was dry. She tried hard to swallow while opening her eyes. Beate was leaning over her, waving her hand in front of her face.

"Four," Victoria mumbled. She sat up slowly, and when Beate handed her a glass of water she drank it in small sips. The fire had almost burned out and, besides Victoria and Beate, only Fi and Bill were left in the living room.

When they noticed that Victoria was awake, Fi quickly came over and put her hand on her forehead. "She's burning hot!" Fi looked at Bill Backsteps.

Bill grabbed her hand.

"Did you see your journey?" he asked.

"I don't know. Maybe?" She tried to think clearly. She wanted to describe her dream to Bill. But instead of listening and helping her understand the dream, Bill gestured for her to stop.

"I cannot help you from here. Your journey is entirely your own. But I am certain you will find your way, because I felt the blood of a thunderbird rushing through your veins."

That night, Beate told Victoria that the elders had also debated politics at the pow wow. "I didn't understand all of it," Beate said, while pulling her nightie on. "But there is something going on that they find utterly unacceptable."

"Can you be a little more precise?" Victoria mumbled from beneath her heavy duvet.

"Well it's got something to do with the climate and global warming. It was something about the Canadian government accepting hazardous waste from other countries. The waste was going to be stored in a deserted part of some Indian territory until it could be properly handled. The Indians interpret the decision as retribution for their lobbying against the government's environmental policy. But they were all very agitated, and it was hard to keep track of the conversation. They also spoke about the consequences of having an oil pipe run all the way from Canada to the States. At one point, I was afraid they were going to dig up the old war hatchet," Beate laughed, jumping head first into her pile of pillows and duvets.

Chapter 12
The Legend

Pennfield, 21 December 2017

Dear Diary,

My grandparents summoned the tribal elders for a pow wow last night and, even though it was very short notice, they all came. Beate and I thought it was all very exciting. The elders were dressed in traditional Indian clothes made of suede and they wore pearls, jewelry and colorful feathers.

It was a wonderful sight☺.

I felt like I had gone back in time.

This morning I phoned my mom and John. Obviously, I didn't tell them that a strange woman had attacked me, and that a spirit from the underworld had tried to kill me!

They would have told me to get on the first plane home!

Instead, I told them about the sweat lodge and the pow wow. Although my dad was Indian, my mother doesn't know much about the Indian ways. And John doesn't either. They liked hearing from me, but seemed more interested in news about me rather than things they cannot really understand.

Then Jeremy called☺.

He suggested some places he thought Beate and I ought to see during our visit. But the mere thought of him made me all giddy, and I could hardly concentrate on what he was saying. All in all, it was a pretty awkward conversation. At the end I told him that I wasn't really feeling well and didn't have the energy to go exploring☹.

Anyway…any relationship is doomed from the beginning. We live on different continents, and I honestly don't know much about all those climate issues that he's so into. Of course, I HAVE heard of the greenhouse effect. And of course I'm against it☺.

It is just not a topic I have been especially interested in. I think I have been too occupied by my own sad situation to worry about climate issues, but it would be super embarrassing if he found out.

Also Jeremy doesn't know that I have the crystal gene, so he doesn't understand why Diane stabbed me with the needle, and I'm not sure how much I should tell him.

Beate, of course, didn't understand why I wouldn't meet with Jeremy. She says I must have blown a fuse during the pow wow☺.

Fi has been treating me with her special ointment, and my wounds are already looking much better, but it might still be a while before my arm gets back to normal. If it ever does. I happened to notice a certain look on her face when she was talking to Charles about the treatment. It was a look that said I was lucky to still have both my arms!

By the way, I asked Fi what 'wisaweyu nipawset macehe' *meant. It was something like 'turn away from the yellow moon'.*

Victoria and Beate were in the living room drinking tea. Outside the windows, big snowflakes were now falling quietly.

"So, you were up in the air, your body covered in feathers. You came close to crashing into a giant rock shaped like a head. And the head opened its mouth to eat you?" Beate recited.

Victoria nodded in confirmation. "If you leave the eating part out. It was like it wanted to invite me in."

"That dream makes absolutely no sense!" Beate said in frustration. "It brings us no closer to understanding how this thunderbird business works. Some help that pow wow gave us!"

"I don't understand it either," Victoria sighed.

She leaned forward to get a piece of the cake Fi had baked earlier that day. "Bill said that they can't help me anymore. It's something I have to figure out for myself." She nibbled the cake. It was a chocolate brownie with bits of orange in it.

"To sum it up, I'm on my own, in a faraway country, having to figure out an ancient rite of passage that got my dad killed. And the fact that they never found his body makes it even worse. I used to have nightmares about it. That he fell into a ravine or was attacked by a wild animal—by a bear, or an American elk, perhaps. As a matter of fact, I still have those dreams." Her voice faded away.

For a moment, neither of them spoke. Beate wanted to comfort her, but she didn't know how.

"About your dream vision. Let's try to look at it in a scientific manner. Analyze it Sherlock-Holmes style, let's carefully examine every detail and every possibility."

Victoria nodded. "Maybe I'm meant to find a place with a colony of big black birds?"

"And what about the water and the head-shaped rock formation? Maybe we are looking for a place with high cliffs close to water?"

"I would say that goes for pretty much

everywhere up here!" giggled Victoria. "But okay, let me think. There was water and cliffs. I had the rising sun behind me. Maybe that tells us something about the direction. In my dream I was flying west, so presumably the rocks we're looking for will be facing east, right?"

"Yes, that must be it! That means that we are looking for some huge cliffs, facing east, and a nesting place for some big black birds. Maybe there is a local version of the guillemots on the Faroe Islands?"

Beate grabbed Fi's laptop and opened Google Earth.

"Let's start with the water. Try moving the map to the left. What do you see?"

"Saint Croix Bay. After that, the water stretches all the way to the Great Lakes. But the shore of Saint Croix Bay is mostly covered with trees, not cliffs."

"Wait! Quoddy Head, with the visitors' center, is more or less west—and a bit to the south. Maybe the sun wasn't directly behind me." Victoria looked thoughtful.

Beate zoomed in on the map and nodded enthusiastically.

"According to Mary Joan, Quoddy Head is a

special place for the Passamaquoddy tribe. It was around the small islands and peninsulas in Passamaquoddy Bay that most of the myths about the god Glooskap unfolded!" Beate jumped from the couch. "Maybe even the legend about the thunderbirds?"

Victoria could feel her heartbeat racing. "I flew in a circle across the water, and then there was another coastline. Maybe it was an island?" Victoria put an uncertain finger on Grand Manan in the sea outside Saint Croix Bay. "But that's probably too far south. Maybe it wasn't an island. Maybe I just flew over a bay?" She ran her finger up the screen until it hit land again on Campobello Island—just across from Quoddy Head. "Actually it could have been the waters leading to the north shore of Quoddy Head. Or the small bay right there, on the south side of Campobello. What does the coastline look like?"

Beate zoomed in closer and switched from map to satellite View.

"It looks like an ordinary beach. Mostly sand! But the one north of Quoddy Head looks pretty rocky," Beate observed.

Victoria nodded.

"It's Quoddy Head! But how do we get there? It

will take hours in this weather, and the road runs inland. How do we even get to the coast?"

"Maybe we could sail? I've read somewhere that warm currents from the sea keep the water ice-free out there. And a boat would definitely be the best way to explore a coastline!" Beate said. "I wonder if Jeremy has access to a boat."

"I'll call him," Victoria said. She grabbed her phone, speed dialed his number and put the speaker on so Beate could listen too. When Victoria heard his voice, her heart started pounding uncontrollably.

It turned out that Jeremy's father had a boat. It was a small cutter, which they used for fishing. Sometimes, Jeremy and his brother even made some extra pocket money by taking tourists out on scenic tours.

"But I don't understand why you want to go to Quoddy Head?"

"During the pow wow at my grandparents' house, I went on a spiritual journey. Unfortunately, the clues are difficult to interpret. But I did get the feeling that Quoddy Head is important to me, and that I should go there," Victoria answered.

She felt divided.

She had told him the truth, but not the whole story.

"Obviously, I wouldn't miss the chance of

spending a whole day with two interesting and beautiful ladies," Jeremy said, and paused.

Victoria felt paralyzed. She tried to think of clever and witty things to say, but the right words did not come.

"Uh…well…" she began, but Beate interrupted her.

"The chance of a lifetime, if you ask me. And you left out 'special'!"

"Yes, you're special too," he said, and laughed. "Otherwise you wouldn't be invited to a pow wow with the elders," Jeremy admitted.

"That's because Diane attacked me," said Victoria.

"Crazy woman that one. It doesn't make any sense at all. I mean, she didn't even know you!" Jeremy paused. He was upset as well as puzzled.

"You're right. It was crazy," Victoria said. She turned to Beate and made a grimace.

"Anyhow, about the sailing trip. Have you asked Fi and Charles for permission?" Jeremy asked.

"No, not yet. But I'll go ask them now and call you back." Victoria said.

"I'll keep my fingers crossed," he grinned and hung up.

"Let's go downstairs," she said to Beate.

"Sightseeing from a boat in the middle of winter doesn't sound like such a good idea," Charles said, and Fi agreed.

"But we're not going sightseeing, it has to do with Victoria's dream vision," Beate explained.

"Really, how is that?" Charles asked.

The girls explained how they had tried to analyze the vision.

"Well, it's an interesting perspective," Charles said, "but I have to talk to Bill Backsteps and Peter Two Hawks about it. I'll call them right away."

About an hour later, Charles called for Victoria and Beate to join them in the kitchen.

"We agree that you should go. Jeremy is an able seaman and even though it's winter, the ocean currents keep the coast around Quoddy Head free from ice.

"It's the Gulf Stream, right?" Beate said, looking knowledgeable.

"I'm impressed!" Charles said. "And, its meeting with the colder Labrador Current just outside Nova Scotia also keeps the waters in motion."

The next morning, the small cutter belonging to the Two Hawks family slowly approached the small harbor at Saint George. The village of Saint George was positioned at the bottom of the bay, just six miles from Pennfield. Every year, the harbor, and the wild river leading through the village and into the bay, attracted hordes of tourists.

Victoria and Beate were waiting on the quay. Jeremy had hardly docked before they jumped on board.

"I am so looking forward to this," exclaimed Victoria tossing her bag into the small cabin.

"It's going to be a great day!" smiled Jeremy. "I've got homemade lemonade, and Storm made us a heap of sandwiches for the trip. My brother is a genius in the kitchen!"

"Great! Why didn't he come too?"

"He wanted to, but unfortunately he had already made other plans. But he asked me to say hello."

They sat on the small deck watching the snow-clad landscape pass them by on both sides, their hot breath creating clouds of steam around them. Soon they reached the calm waters of the bay. Jeremy looked as if he was enjoying the outing—he couldn't stop smiling. Mostly at Victoria, but Beate also got a few traffic-stopping smiles.

Beate leaned over the side of the boat. The water was so clear that she could see the bottom of the boat.

"The surface is like a mirror! I thought the currents kept the water in constant motion?" Beate said.

"The currents run deeper." Jeremy said. "Up here you hardly notice it."

Eventually, the last bit of haze lifted. There wasn't a cloud in the sky, and you could clearly see the nearby coastline.

Victoria looked up. She closed her eyes and felt the warm rays from the sun on her cheeks. "This is great," she sighed.

"Look!" Beate said and pointed into the water. "How cute is that?" She had spotted a small whale surfacing to breathe.

They sailed alongside the whale until it disappeared in the bluish-green waters.

"I've never seen anything like it. It was so close I could have touched it!" Beate said, and let her hand water ski on the surface.

"Oh shoot, we should have taken a picture," Victoria said, but it was too late, the whale had gone.

Jeremy steered the cutter south toward the mouth of the bay and Quoddy Head.

"Do you know the story about Big Bear and Little Bear?" asked Victoria.

"I certainly do." Jeremy smiled, leaning against the

rail. With a gentle hand on the wheel, he started telling the story. "Once there were these thunderbirds. The thunderbirds were the people of the sky. They lived in a secret cave, where they kept many old scriptures containing most of the knowledge they had accumulated through the centuries. They had many enemies, and among them the Wolf Spirit, called Loks. The Bear Spirit was also at war with Loks, and so the thunderbirds and the Bear Spirit combined forces against the Wolf Spirit. But there was a problem. When the thunderbirds flew into battle, their cave was left unprotected. Therefore, the Spirit Bear sent two spirits to guard the cave. They were called Big Bear and Little Bear. The Spirit Bear created two figurines to house the spirits, and placed them at the entrance of the secret cave.

"Big Bear and Little Bear became the guardians of the thunderbirds' cave. The bear spirits ensured that only friendly spirits, and people belonging to the thunderbird bloodline, were allowed to enter the cave." Jeremy stopped talking for a minute while he steered the cutter around a floating log.

"According to the myths, the cave was also the place where new thunderbirds underwent their initiations and were awarded their wings. No one knows the location of the cave though. That is, if it even exists."

"Mary Joan thinks that she has acquired one of the bear figurines," said Victoria.

"Honestly—it's just an old legend. People of the thunderbird bloodline? Just try saying it out loud!" He grimaced. "But, kids in this part of Canada still dress up as thunderbirds alongside Marvel superheroes and, if they break a leg, they hope that their genes will turn out to be special." He smiled.

Victoria and Beate exchanged glances.

"Maybe there is more to the world than meets the eye," said Beate.

Jeremy shrugged, "Some of the elders are still waiting for the next thunderbird to appear. The tribes do much better whenever there is a thunderbird. But as far as I know, there hasn't been any stories of thunderbirds in at least a hundred years, and they should be easy enough to spot! Actually, my father used to joke about your father having the crystal gene. He was a wild child who kept breaking his arms and legs!"

Jeremy mistook Victoria's troubled look for surprise. "You didn't know?"

"Of course I did. He suffered from osteoporosis

just like me," Victoria said.

"So you don't believe the legends?" asked Beate quickly.

Jeremy hesitated while considering his answer.

Finally he said, "It's part of my cultural heritage, so I don't question the stories. But it's the older generations that keep the legends alive. It makes no difference to me whether the legends are true or not. They're a part of our past, and a part of me." He seemed very confident with his answer. "But what is with you two, and all these questions about the thunderbird?"

"It's a part of my past too!" Victoria said. Why was it so hard to understand? "We want to know the history of my dad's tribe!"

Jeremy gave both the girls a long look. Then he nodded and turned his attention to steering the boat.

It took about an hour to get to Quoddy Head. Everywhere the coastline was covered in powdered snow. Green pine trees lined the bank behind the cliffs. Together they formed an impenetrable wall of white, grey and green.

A large bird shrieked as it soared toward the sky. Otherwise, the place was still, as if the snow muffled all sounds. When Jeremy turned the engine off the silence seemed almost artificial.

The boat slowly rocked on the water's mirror-like surface. Victoria and Beate winced against the bright sunlight reflected by the snow as they peered along the coastline. But there was no rock shaped like a giant Indian head—no cave, not even a dark opening, to be seen anywhere.

"Can we go around that outcrop?" Victoria suggested. "Maybe we'll get a better view from there."

Jeremy started the engine back up and sailed around the point.

The girls screened the coastline carefully, but they didn't find anything resembling a giant head, not even a tiny crack that could be the entrance to a cave.

"Can we get ashore somehow?" asked Beate.

Jeremy looked surprised.

"Ashore? Here? No, that wouldn't be possible! Maybe further down, but then we'd have to go back through the forest to get to the shore. And there are no paths in there. With all that snow...it could take hours."

"Never mind," said Victoria. "It isn't here anyway!"

"What isn't here?" Jeremy asked.

The girls didn't answer.

Jeremy turned off the engine. "Listen up," he

said. "This is how it's going to be: either you tell me what this is really about, or I'll turn the boat around and go straight back to the harbor."

Victoria tried to look surprised, but Jeremy just shook his head.

"I've played along so far, but there is clearly something going on. Spill it!"

"We're looking for Victoria's Indian!" Beate blurted out. "Oh no," she said, and covered her mouth with her hand.

For a moment, Jeremy just stared at Beate. Then he burst into laughter and turned to Victoria. "You are out here looking for an Indian guy? I really appreciate the obvious lack of competition on the boat, but instead of all the old stories about the thunderbirds, I probably should have told you more about contemporary Indian traditions. You can marry whoever you want!" He winked at Victoria.

"No, silly," said Victoria. She felt her entire face blushing. "I'm not here to find a husband!"

"Of course you're not," Jeremy said, "but that's exactly my point! Why are you here? Why are we here—on this boat? It's time you come clean and tell me what this is all about!"

"Okay," Victoria took a deep breath, "we don't

believe the legends about the thunderbirds are just myths. In fact, we believe that the myths are true!" Victoria paused and looked at Jeremy.

Jeremy didn't say a word. He just stood at the wheel and looked at the water with a distant expression on his face.

Victoria wondered if he thought she was immature. Sixteen years old and still believing in elves and fairies.

The silence was insufferable. She looked at Beate, who gestured for her to pinch him. Funny! Victoria shook her head at Beate, took another deep breath, and decided to break the spell.

"During the pow wow at my grandparents' house, I went on a spiritual journey. But the clues are really difficult to interpret. In the dream I saw a rock that looked like the head of a giant Indian. We need to find that Indian head and we think that it might be somewhere around here. So, we've come to look for answers. But, so far, I don't see anything that can be linked to the images in my dream." She looked at him. "Do you think I'm crazy? Ready for hospitalization?"

"Who decides who's crazy?" said Jeremy. "The Indian culture is my life. It's in my bones. But until a few days ago I never thought that the myths were anything but bedtime stories. If anyone had asked me if I believed in them, I would have dismissed the idea—without hesitation. Now I don't know. Diane must have had a reason to attack you. I guess the needle was smothered in poison since it made you ill. But Bill Backsteps saved you. How did he know what to do? He's a medicine man, not a doctor, and it makes me think that perhaps there is more to the world if you open your mind. And, as I said earlier today, I recognize that...you're someone special. Someone of great value to your tribe." He winked at her. "Besides, old Bill Backsteps doesn't come into town for just any tourist, and my father never lets us take the boat out in winter. So no, I don't think you are crazy! Or at least I don't think you've been diagnosed yet," he said with a grin.

"Whereas I'm sure Beate is."

"Smartass!" Beate said with a loud sniff.

"So, we are here because you had a dream vision— and, in that dream vision, there was a rock shaped like an Indian head?" He put his arm around Victoria, just as he had done that day in the sweat lodge.

Victoria calmed herself, hoping he wouldn't notice her heart skipping a beat. The same way it had almost betrayed her feelings that first night.

She cleared her throat. "Bingo! We're looking for a rock shaped like a giant Indian head. We think the head will lead us to the cave."

He smiled. "The thunderbirds' secret cave?"

Victoria nodded.

"I am afraid I am going to have to disappoint you. I have never seen a cave or a grotto around these waters. And we've done quite a lot of fishing in this area."

"Are you sure?" Victoria said.

Jeremy nodded.

She had had high hopes for this trip, and now she suddenly had no energy left. It was all very disappointing.

"Well let's go back then," Victoria said.

Jeremy swung the wheel around so the bow pointed straight north. Then he accelerated the boat.

"Wait," said Victoria. "Could we sail back along a different route? Maybe go south of Campobello Island? I'd like to see the bay now that we're here anyway."

"That's a good idea," said Beate. "It's such a beautiful landscape, let's see some more of it."

"No problem," Jeremy said. He changed course and they sailed eastward into Fundy Bay.

The boat moved slowly up the coast, with Victoria and Beate standing at the bow like two decorative figureheads.

"Annnnd right around the corner, the famooooous Herring Cove Beach...." Jeremy was trying his best to sound like a tourist guide when Beate interrupted him, calling out excitedly, "Stop!"

Jeremy and Victoria both looked at Beate.

"There!" Beate pointed directly toward a dark feature in the white snow. "See? Could that be it?" In her eagerness to get a good look, Victoria almost went over the side of the boat. Silhouetted against the white snow, a dark rock did, in fact, resemble the profile of a head. A big nose. Eyebrows. A pointy chin. The closer they got, the more it looked like the image from her dream.

"Can we go in there?" she asked.

But Jeremy was already heading toward the shore.

"I've never noticed that rock formation before," he said in surprise. "But I agree. It really looks like a giant Indian head. Let's take a look!"

Right below the cliffs was a small beach—with great skill Jeremy sailed the small cutter as close to the shore as humanly possible.

"Imagine being so happy about wearing Wellingtons!" Victoria said. "But the water sure looks cold."

Jeremy had brought the cutter within a few yards from the beach, and they all eased into the cold low water. On dry land, waves had washed away the snow and they easily reached the giant rock.

They looked at the Indian head.

"This is it," Victoria said. "This is the image from my dream vision!" She felt fresh energy soaring through her veins.

"We found it!" Beate hooted and started performing a self-composed war dance in front of the giant rock.

"And now what?" Jeremy looked at the steep surface rising above them. "You're not considering climbing that, are you?"

"Definitely not, because that would be insane!" Beate said, giving Victoria a hard look.

Victoria knitted her brows as she often did while making important decisions. "I have a job to do, and I need to do it on my own. The two of you will have to wait here."

"I don't think this is a good idea," Jeremy said.

"I agree," Beate said. "It's too dangerous. Especially for you!"

"I don't care! I have come too far to give up at this point. The Carpathians sent a spirit from the underworld to kill me, and they will keep trying to get to me!" Victoria said.

Like a hero in front of a firing squad, she straightened up with an embattled look in her eyes. "This is our chance to strike back and I'm not going to quit!"

"The Carpathians? Spirits from the underworld? What are you talking about?" Jeremy flung his arms out in the air.

"It has to do with the myths! I promise we'll tell you all about it later. Right now, I'm going to climb that rock, and I have to do it on my own!"

"I have a bad feeling about this," Beate said.

"Please go. I promise I will be careful. I won't do anything foolish or reckless," Victoria pleaded.

Jeremy saw the fire burning in Victoria's eyes. Then he pointed in the direction of the cutter. "I guess that's the way it has to be. We'll keep ourselves warm in the cabin. Please take care, Victoria. Icy stone surfaces can cause broken limbs, or worse."

The expression on their faces, as they started wading back to the cutter, clearly showed that they were not sure whether to trust her or not.

But Victoria was sure. No one could help her

from this point on.

This was her journey.

She spun around and determinedly approached the giant head's pointy stone chin.

Chapter 13
The Indian Head

THE NARROW STRIP of beach ended abruptly at the foot of the cliffs. The rock in front of Victoria was massive, and stood at least 15 feet tall. Above it, she could see the snow-covered tops of the tall pines, and behind her was the sea.

It was strange seeing the large Indian head in real life. In her dream vision, the Indian had looked straight at her. Now the eyes were grey granite, they peered blindly across the bay.

What was she supposed to do now?

She had hoped that finding the Indian head would provide some kind of epiphany. After all, she had solved the riddle presented to her on her spiritual journey.

Nothing happened. There were no further instructions from above telling her what to do next.

In her dream vision, the open mouth could have resembled the entrance to a cave, but, close up, the giant rock was just a massive lump of granite. Maybe the entrance to the cave was concealed in the cliffs behind it?

The surface of the Indian face was partly covered in snow and very slippery. She put one foot on the chin, stretched and grabbed hold of the upper lip and, with a mighty heave, she succeeded in pulling herself up, so that she could position her other foot on the lower lip. She placed her knee on the upper lip and reached for the nose, but her weak left hand failed her. She slipped and swung around, banging herself hard on the rock. A sharp pain shot through her side, and she remembered that there was a reason she didn't usually go mountain climbing. She let herself slide back down until she reached solid ground. Her hip hurt. Maybe it was just a sprain. That is, if you could even sprain a hip. She tried to dismiss the thought, but already she could feel her confidence failing.

Light clouds moved across the sky. They cast shadows that made it seem like the Indian head was grinning at her.

Mocking her.

She studied the face. The square protruding chin, the furrowed lips, the curved cheeks and the long bridge of the nose. There was nothing to hang on to. Ascent was impossible.

In frustration, she picked up a stone and threw it

as far into the water as she could. It disappeared with a small plop. There was nothing to be done, so she started limping back toward the boat. She picked out her phone. It was in her inside pocket and must have hit the rock when she was swung around, but it looked all right. She tried to call Beate to tell her that she was coming, but there was no signal.

So close, and yet so far away.

It was like old times. Before the trip to Dresden. Back when she had spent most of her time with broken and bandaged limbs. She had failed because she was weak!

"I'm so WEAK!" she yelled out, kicking at the ground. "Weak...weak...weak...." Even the echo from the cliffs mocked her. She turned angrily toward the echo.

What was that? A tear in the corner of an eye?

An eye made of stone glistened with tears.

How was that possible?

She limped back to get a better look. It had to be melting snow, but it looked decidedly like tears!

While Victoria was watching, more tears melted the snow under the eyes. She noticed a small pool where the tears gathered before flowing down the nose.

Was that a *dimple*?

She hadn't noticed it before.

She watched the tears pool, and then draw a visible track down the face. The route ended at her feet.

Victoria gritted her teeth and stepped up onto the chin again. This time, she stretched, and grabbed onto a small ledge in the route cleared by the melting snow.

This could be the way!

Again, she placed one foot on the lower lip, her knee on the upper lip, and heaved herself up. She clung to the slippery rock like a fly while her foot searched for traction. Jabs of pain shot through her hip.

She found another foothold in the snow-cleared track. She curled up, and pushed off while she grabbed onto the nose with her weak left hand.

The pain made her eyesight blurry, and she struggled to hang on. She had to calm herself. She took a long, deep breath. Then she carefully placed her right foot in the nostril. With a firm grip on the dimple, and one knee on the nose, she managed to heave herself up. She stepped on the cheekbone, and swung herself around to the ear by holding on to an eyebrow. From the ear, she stepped back onto the eyebrow and, using the forehead as a stepping stone, she leaped to the top of the head.

She slipped down on the other side and curled up against the Indian's neck.

She had made it.

She had climbed the face.

So far so good.

Victoria's entire body ached and her legs were trembling. However, the feeling of success and the knowledge of being one step closer drove her on. She stood up and looked around.

There was a path—nothing more than an animal track—leading between the cliffs toward the pine trees. She followed the track for a while. Just before she reached the pines, the cliffs turned into a tall wall of slippery rock. The wall was too steep to climb and instead the track turned away from the forest and continued along the coast, slowly ascending until it ended, abruptly, at a drop of at least 15 feet.

What now?

She looked around, and then she saw it.

Between two large boulders was an opening. It was a very small opening, half hidden under a mantle of snow. It looked like a shelter for animals. Could this really be it?

The pain in her hip was almost unbearable as she

heaved herself along and stretched up to the opening. She poked her head in. Inside was dark, yet she sensed that the place was big enough for a person to stand upright.

Her heart was beating fast with excitement when she pushed her way through the opening. She turned on her phone's flashlight and looked around. She found herself in a narrow grotto. The air felt dry, and there was sand on the floor. The sand felt soft beneath her feet as she limped onward.

About 50 feet down the grotto, she found another, larger opening. She felt a jolt. Right in front of her was the silhouette of a giant bear. It had been sculpted into the very rock. Its enormous paws were raised and ready to strike. Its mouth was half open, and frozen in a snarl, revealing long, pointy teeth. Half hidden in the dark its eyes seemed to gleam menacingly—as if containing a hidden camera that secretly zoomed in on its prey.

For a brief moment, it seemed like the air itself shimmered before her while the bear figurine silently watched its guest.

She swallowed hard.

"Hello there. You must be Big Bear." Her voice trembled slightly. The figurine was very lifelike. "I know that you're meant to ward off evil, so I sincerely hope you can see that I am one of the good guys!" She hesitated for a moment.

Then she stepped forward.

A sharp pain shot through her shoulder and into her injured arm, knocking the wind out of her. Then the bear released its hold on her, and she tumbled into the cave.

She wheezed.

She had felt Big Bear's power. And it seemed to have had second thoughts about letting her in. Could it maybe sense the remnants of the evil spirit that had clawed her arm?

Or was she still marked by the sacrificial needle?

Not a pleasant thought.

She straightened up and looked around. She was surrounded by steep cave walls. In the ceiling were small cracks where streams of daylight peered through. It wasn't much, but now she was able to see without using the flashlight on her phone. She pocketed the phone and looked around curiously. The walls were decorated with colorful paintings portraying birds and Indians. Along the far side, a shelf had been chiseled into the wall. The shelf contained bones, feathers, small bouquets of herbs and flowers, sealed jars, empty clay pots and handwritten parchments. It was obvious that they had been organized to suit some unknown purpose.

A cooking vessel was hanging above a burnt-out fireplace. In the back of the cave, a small spring trickled. The water flowed through narrow cracks in the floor and through an opening in the cave wall, where it disappeared over a small ledge like a waterfall.

It seemed that time had been standing still in the grotto. Victoria couldn't shake the feeling that whoever had been there last was still around. However, all the items on the shelf were covered in a thick layer of dust. No one had been there for a very long time.

The paintings on the walls portrayed an Indian in different situations. Almost like a cartoon strip, Victoria thought. At first, he sat at a table mixing something. Then he stood by a waterfall, and then next to a fireplace. At the end, he was maybe swimming or hovering in a horizontal position.

Victoria took a step backward. It looked as if he was portrayed above the small ledge outside the cave.

She hobbled to the small opening and looked outside. The ledge was only ten feet long and no more than three feet wide. It was a ledge leading nowhere.

Victoria stepped outside onto the ledge, and looked down. It was at least 20 feet to the bottom of an almost circular crater. The sides of the crater were made of tall cliffs, interrupted only by a group of dark pines on the inland side. The bottom was strewn with sharp and pointy rocks.

On the far side of the surrounding cliffs, she noticed another wall painting—two giant half circles in yellow paint. The half circles were identical, but mirrored.

Not an easy place to paint something. So what was it all about? It was all very exciting, but first she had to focus on the wall paintings inside the cave. If she was to follow the steps displayed, the ledge seemed to be last in line. Could it be that the paintings illustrated the making of the potion?

In the middle of the cave was a small outcrop, about three feet tall. It looked as if it had grown straight up from the cave floor. The shape of the outcrop made her think of a Christmas tree.

Standing as she did, outside on the ledge, the Christmas-tree rock effectively blocked her view of the first image on the wall positioned right inside the entrance, next to Big Bear.

Sidestepping on the ledge to get a full view of the paintings, she noticed a rhythmic humming sound. It sounded like a swarm of grasshoppers.

Step by step she neared the edge of the ledge. A foot from the edge, the humming sound turned into a howling storm, tearing at her eardrums, hair and clothes.

It was a natural phenomenon that created the rhythmic sounds and hard winds. When the powerful gusts from the sea were pushed against the cliffs, they were driven through cracks and crevices in the granite, gaining power on their way—until finally emerging next to the ledge with enormous force.

Victoria felt the raw strength of the wind and was overwhelmed with fear. She had to hold onto a protruding stone to keep the wind from pulling her off the ledge and down into the crater.

The thought of Beate and Jeremy crossed her mind. She had promised to be careful, but now she was standing on the edge of a cliff, clinging to its stone surface, in danger of getting blown down into a deep crater!

Was she out of her mind?

She felt terrified.

She had to calm down.

Slowly, she counted to ten, breathing in deeply at every count. She used a firm tone to tell herself that everything was under control!

Then she gazed around and noticed that, from this position—on the far left side of the ledge—she could look into the cave and finally see all the wall paintings at the same time.

From this angle, instead of blocking her view, it actually looked as if the Christmas-tree rock was now pointing to one of the paintings.

If one was to start reading the cartoon from there, she would have to fly *before* making the potion. She sighed. How could that be? Surely, it had to be the potion that made flying possible?

She turned her back on the cave and peered down into the crater. The pointy rocks at the bottom were a scary sight. A particularly tall one stood out, it had very sharp and jagged edges.

The mere thought of falling made her dizzy, but this time she managed to control her fear. She turned around and focused on the painting of the flying Indian.

What was he doing with his arms?

Flapping?

Swimming?

Waving?

Was the red bit in the middle, in fact, the tall, pointy rock below? The shape looked just about right, but the color was wrong. Was the rock covered in blood?

Her legs were shaking and it wasn't just because of the strong winds trying to pull her away from the ledge.

She breathed in deeply, and focused on the ledge. She stood on the very edge, with the rhythmic concert of the howling winds all around her. It reminded her of the humming sound from the pow wow at her grandparents' house. Only this time it was much louder.

She crouched down, closed her eyes, and let her mind travel back. She thought about the sound that the elders had produced. It had surrounded her, and had almost felt tangible enough to carry her, if it had somehow been possible for her to step onto it.

She opened her eyes.

Could this sound really carry her?

Or could the wind?

Was that it?

Was she supposed to just step into the wind?

Victoria stood up.

This would be nothing short of suicide.

She felt herself swaying on the ledge.

Her hip and her left arm were aching, and she felt immensely exhausted. She imagined the Indian head by the beach. In the dream, it had winked at her and opened its mouth to let her in. There was more to life than what could be seen by the naked eye. If nothing else, her journey had taught her that.

She let go of the small, protruding stone and stepped into the wind.

Chapter 14
The Ritual

SHE DID NOT FALL.

Instead, the wind carried her straight toward the spiky rock in the middle of the crater.

She was moving fast. Its sharp, rugged edges would cut her to pieces for sure.

At the very last moment, she was lifted up past the sharp rock, but now she was heading straight toward the far side of the crater.

The strong wind made her eyes water and even breathing was difficult. Adrenalin was pumping through her body.

For a brief second she suddenly thought of Beate's sketch. She realized that the Indian in the picture was flying above this very same tall, pointy rock.

She began to sway and flap her arms about like a bird. It was not very efficient, but slowly she began moving away from the edge of the crater. The tall rock provided shelter from the whirling wind, and she managed to steer herself behind its protective mass. Her speed was slowed until she hung motionless in mid-air. Currents of wind, bouncing off the crater walls and gusting straight up in a powerful vertical motion, held her up.

Victoria tried to balance herself in the wind. Slowly, she rose upward toward the crater mouth. Again, she saw the two yellow half circles. Only from this angle, they seemed to have joined into one large circle.

Was it a sun?

Or maybe a full moon?

Victoria knew straight away that the circle was important. She remembered the sentence the old woman had said to her repeatedly at the pow wow. Fi had translated it for her. It was something about turning away from the yellow moon....

She flapped her arms and managed to swivel around, turning her back on the yellow circle to face the cave while she continued her ascent. Then it hit her. She had been here before.

In a dream.

Or rather, in a nightmare.

Back in Denmark. On the day she had received Beate's letter.

It felt like a lifetime ago.

She recognized the cliff, the trees, and the whispered warning. In the nightmare, she had been drawn toward the looming pines, where darkness had consumed her.

Now, she was sure she had to stay clear of the pines.

She had barely finished the thought before the current of wind rising behind the massive body of the spiky rock split in two. One current pushed her toward the trees, and the other in the direction of the ledge.

It was almost as if the two currents of wind were fighting over her. She flapped her arms and legs as best she could, but the trees were winning. Like anglers, they patiently pulled in their net.

It was exactly like in her nightmare.

The panic she was feeling was almost physically crippling.

Turning her flapping arms into random twitches.

In a few seconds, the current would push her away from the updraft, and she would be crushed against the cliffs below the trees. With one last effort, she reached out, grabbing onto the tall rock. Its sharp edges cut her fingers, but she managed to hang on.

With her last strength, she pulled herself into the safer current of wind. The one that would take her back to the ledge.

All the pieces were there. The Indian head, the

cave, the dark trees and the yellow moon.

And it was all over.

All her energy was gone and she was none the wiser.

Like a puppet, she was slowly carried back toward the cave. She passed the spot where the half circles joined and, feeling a bit embarrassed, she looked down—and away from the yellow moon.

Then she discovered something.

From her vantage point in the middle of the crater, she could see some symbols chiseled into the cliff above the ledge.

She didn't quite understand what they meant, but she managed to memorize the combination of the various symbols before the wind carefully placed her back on the ledge. Then her weary body gave way, and she almost rolled onto the floor of the cave.

She got up.

Light-headed, she realized that she had made it.

She was still alive!

She had passed the test!

It had been exactly like the illustrations in Beate's sketch. Young Indians, like herself, who were trying to uncover the secrets of the thunderbird.

And many of them had not made it.

But she had!

She threw her arms in the air triumphantly and, just for a brief moment, the cave resounded with an alternative version of Queen's 'We Are the Champions'.

* * *

Slowly, her joy and excitement were replaced by worry.

What had she actually achieved?

Besides the honor?

She was sitting on the floor of a hidden cave. In the middle of nowhere. Far away from Beate and Jeremy. She was exhausted and injured, and the pain made it almost impossible to move. How was she going to get back?

And there was no way that Beate and Jeremy could help her. They had no chance of finding her here. Even if they succeeded in climbing the Indian head, they probably wouldn't be able to get past Big Bear and enter the grotto.

She was overwhelmed by fatigue and pain. She was so beat that she didn't even realize she was crying until she tasted salty tears on her lips.

She leaned back against the wall.

There had to be some greater meaning to it all!

For a while, she sat there quietly. Then she tried

to pull herself together.

The old Indians would help her along!

She sniffed, and dried her tears. Then she focused on the wall paintings. They had to be the key. She was sure of it. All she had to do was figure it out.

There were two paintings in the cartoon she hadn't deciphered yet. One was the alchemist Indian. He was sitting on the floor, mixing things in a clay jar. She wanted to get up, but her legs wouldn't carry her. Instead, she crawled toward the wall. With a firm grip on the shelf, she managed to stand up. One by one, she looked into the many jars. She was supposed to make a potion, but how?

There were leaves, flowers, seeds, powdered stuff, feathers, bones, crystals and much more. Where to begin?

She stroked the soft feathers with her fingertips. They had probably been very colorful once. Over time they had lost their glow under a thick layer of dust. She used the feathers to dust the shelf. Some written symbols appeared. They had been chipped into the shelf next to a jar of herbs.

A burst of energy came over her as she continued to sweep away the dust. It turned out that there were symbols next to all the items placed on the shelf.

She also discovered a pile of parchment. All the pages were densely printed with Indian symbols.

She gathered those ingredients from the shelf that matched the symbols she had seen above the ledge. She placed them in order accordingly.

Some of the items had sub-symbols. The extra symbols were instructions on how to treat specific ingredients. One could be the small symbol of a mortar, or a chopping knife. Next to a bronze cup were two identical symbols—illustrations of a small stream. That meant adding two cups of water. One by one, she mixed them all in a cooking vessel, according to the amounts described.

Next to the fireplace, she found a lighter of flint, and dry firewood. She remembered her days as a scout when she was younger, and had no difficulty lighting a fire.

While she stirred the soup, her mind raced. Beate and Jeremy were probably worried about her. She only hoped that they had not alerted the coast guard. Then she wondered if her dad had found the cave.

And if he had, then what had happened to him?

The contents of the pot began to congeal into some dark goo. In the end, it resembled the mixture the mad doctor had given her. But, although it looked right, the result was definitely not impressive. The bit that was left, after it had been boiled down, could fit in a pill bottle.

Clearly, she would need more, but she had to worry about that later.

Victoria continued stirring the goo until all the fluid evaporated. Then she used a spoon to scoop the mixture into a small bottle. When she had capped it, she washed the pot by the small stream and placed everything back on the shelf.

She sighed, and sat down on the cold floor to rest.

What to do next? There was only one more panel in the cartoon strip on the wall.

A sitting Indian—his head surrounded by a cloud of strange symbols.

She looked at the small stack of parchment. No doubt they contained more secrets.

As a thunderbird, it was her duty to study them. But how was she to decipher them, and then memorize it all?

She weighed the small jar of mixture in her hand. She would have to use some of it now. Otherwise, she would not have the strength to climb all the way back to the boat. Suddenly, she remembered that one of the effects of the potion had also been to make her acutely perceptive. She had been solving five-star Sudokus in a matter of minutes on the way back from the clinic in Dresden!

Everything was going to be okay.

Eagerly, she dipped her fingers into the jar. The consistency was as revolting as she remembered. She swallowed hard.

For a moment she felt like vomiting. Then, a warm glowing sensation washed over her. Her injured left arm fought the heat briefly, then surrendered to the warm feeling. The glowing sensation soothed her weary bones. She felt a surge of energy ignite each and every fiber of her being— she jumped up.

The ache in her hip had gone.

She rolled up her sleeve. The cuts that had scarred her arm had vanished.

Emotions.

Colors.

Everything exploded in cascades of golden light inside her head.

And right in the middle of it all, she felt her dad's presence.

She didn't know how she knew, but there was no doubt. Maybe he had also passed the test? Whatever had happened to her dad, he had definitely made it to the cave. She could feel it!

In a rush of joy, she danced over to the parchments. Seeing the symbols through the golden glow that now enveloped her world, she had no trouble deciphering them.

It was the wisdom of the thunderbirds, dating back to the making of the world. The symbols described the elements of nature, and how energy was created by upsetting their internal balance. It was powerful knowledge for both good and bad.

When she had finished reading, she placed the pieces of parchment back on the shelf—ready for the next visitor who reached the cave and passed the test.

Maybe fifty, or even a hundred years from now.

Chapter 15
Rings of Fire

New Brunswick, 23 December 2017

Dear Diary,

My experiences in the cave were scary but the results were more than I had ever dared hope for!

Finding the cave, and the test, left my body almost useless. But when I drank the mixture, the pain disappeared like ice cream on a sunny day.

It worked exactly as I remembered it.

All my broken bones healed, and I almost exploded with new energy. I made my way back to the boat in no time. I literally mean no time.

I felt as if I could actually fly☺.

It's powerful stuff☺.

I can't wait to explore all the things I learned from the parchments.

Jeremy and Beate were so relieved to see me. It surprised me a bit, to realize how worried they had been, but it also made me glad☺.

They told me I had been away for hours and, if Jeremy hadn't been there to calm her down, Beate would have used the cutter's radio to call the coastguard.

She later told me that she had even been too worried to flirt with Jeremy, so she really hoped I was finally going to do something about it myself.

Crazy girl☺.

Of course, they wanted to hear all about the cave, and how I had discovered the recipe for the mixture.

I told them everything, but Jeremy was struggling hard to believe my story.

He tried to rationalize the whole thing, saying I had been under a lot of pressure, that I'd crossed the point of no return when I climbed the Indian head with a broken hip. He said the wall paintings, and all the other stuff in the cave, were there because medicine men must have come there for centuries, probably due to the wind phenomenon. And maybe I didn't feel any pain going back to the boat because adrenalin was pumping through my body....

Sometimes Jeremy is really uphill!

Beate, on the other hand, she believed every word.

It's kind of funny when you think of it. She comes from a

country where we don't believe in anything if it hasn't been scientifically proven. Whereas Jeremy has lived his whole life with the Indian ways and beliefs.

Yet he's the one who questions my story.

However, he did realize that he had to be more open minded about all this 'cultural stuff'.

I was a bit worried about what my grandparents would say when they learned how I had involved Jeremy. However, it turned out very well.

My grandfather told me there was no reason to keep secrets from the Two Hawks since they were also part of the Abenaki people. Somehow, that makes us allies! Besides that, my family and his go way back!

It made me very happy☺.

Bill Backsteps wanted to invite everyone for another pow wow, so that the elders could hear me tell my story. However, my grandmother thought it would be too much fuss. I also need to relax and enjoy my vacation, she said.

It's the last night before going back to Denmark, so we've invited our closest friends and relatives for dinner. Unfortunately, Aunt Ann can't make it, but the others are coming. Including Jeremy☺.

It makes me sad to think that we are leaving☹.

Who knows when we'll see them again?

I called Mom and John and told them about all the exciting things I've experienced.

The censored version, of course.

They were a little upset that I hadn't done my blood tests. But I simply forgot☹.

* * *

Fire was raging in the fireplace. Mary Joan, Bill, Jeremy and his father had arrived. They were sitting in Fi and Charle's living room, their shadows dancing on the walls.

"It has been more than a hundred years since the last thunderbird," Bill said. "Until Victoria has finished her training as our new medicine man, we'll all be vulnerable. Victoria's journey has only just begun, and no one here knows where the road might take her. The Carpathians are already on her trail. It seems they have an amazing ability to turn up when you least expect it. So we have to expect the unexpected, and we must do our best to protect her." He turned to Beate. "Can we count on you to help us look after Victoria?"

"That goes without saying!" Beate said. Then she hesitated, "But even though we're best friends, we're not together 24/7!"

"I'm aware of that. Therefore, I would like you to decide on some simple routines. For example, make it a habit to call each other every night to discuss any strange things she may have encountered, and help her make the right choices."

"As if we don't do that already...." Beate interjected, but Bill stopped her.

"Also, I propose that we all get new mobile phones with secret numbers. Numbers only known to our little group, and used for emergencies only. That way we'll know it's important, when one of these numbers calls."

"If anything happens—anything odd or a little too coincidental—you mustn't hesitate to call us," said Fi. She looked at Charles. He nodded. Then she got up and fetched a small leather pouch containing a yellow powder. She poured some of it onto the dining room table, forming a circle. Then she took a box of matches from a drawer and lit a match.

"Hey!" Victoria cried, when she realized what Fi was going to do.

"Don't worry! Just watch!" Fi said calmly, and

put the flaming match to the powder. Immediately, it started spluttering and hissing, burning with poisonous flames.

Fi rolled up her sleeve and slowly ran her arm through the flames. When the flames licked her skin they died down, leaving a glowing orange ring on the table. Then she waved at Victoria to come sit next to her.

"You can always reach us through this ring of fire."

Victoria leaned forward and peered into the dark center of the glowing ring. It looked like a mirror in a golden frame. Slowly the contours of a face appeared.

"Welcome back, Victoria."

To her great surprise, Victoria was staring right into the face of her Aunt Ann, and she could even hear her voice.

"Ann?" Victoria muttered. "Where are you?"

"I am at home. In my kitchen." Ann's voice sounded distant and oddly hollow.

"This is amazing!" Victoria exclaimed.

"We use the ring of fire when we need to talk face-to-face," said Fi.

Victoria, Jeremy and Mary Joan all just sat there, paralyzed.

"A magic ring of fire? Apart from this being way cooler, we already have other, easier ways to video communicate," Beate said.

"I know," Fi said. "It's modern times, but you shouldn't dismiss tradition! And you're in for another surprise!"

"There is more?" Mary Joan asked.

"I've been looking forward to showing you this all day," Fi said as she got up.

Fi looked around, and then took a candlestick from a coffee table. She handed the candlestick through the ring—where Ann took it!

Just as if Ann had been sitting next to them at the table!

Ann tapped the candlestick with a teaspoon to show that it was real. Then she handed it back through the ring!

"I don't think Skype can do that!" Fi said, and put the candlestick back on the coffee table.

"No, Skype can't do THAT!" Beate cheered, and clapped her hands.

"I'm speechless!" Jeremy exclaimed.

"I still remember the day I first saw the spell," Charles said. "It really rocks your world when you realize that our dimension isn't the only one."

"I don't know what to say," Mary Joan said.

"How come you didn't burn yourselves?" Victoria asked, looking from Fi to Ann.

"The flames are only an optical illusion," Ann explained. "You can't feel them at all."

"And that's why the table doesn't burn," Fi intervened.

"You knew about this?" Jeremy asked, looking at his father.

"Yes, son," Peter said.

"And you never told me?"

"I was going to," Peter explained. "But magic is serious stuff. Even I still find it difficult to comprehend."

"Does Mom know about it too?"

His father nodded.

Jeremy sighed. Then he turned to Bill. "You're right about this rocking my world! How do I learn more?"

They all laughed.

"Don't laugh, I also want to learn this!" Beate said.

"Me too!" said Victoria. "Since magic seems to be my new line of work!"

Jeremy grabbed Victoria's hand. "I'm sorry I didn't believe you."

"It's okay. It was a very crazy story!" Victoria said.

"I will join Victoria's ring of protectors too!" Jeremy said in a solemn voice, still holding her hand.

"I'd like that," Victoria said.

"I'll call you soon. On a real phone," Ann said, imitating a phone with her right hand.

"Goodbye dear," Fi said, and started blowing out the flames.

They all waved at Ann.

Then Victoria noticed it. A man was looking at Ann through her kitchen window. Ann—sitting with her back turned to the window—couldn't see him.

"Wait!" Victoria yelled, and jumped out of her seat.

Fi looked at her with surprise. But it was too late. The ring was gone, leaving only a puff of smoke in its wake.

"Did you see him?"

"Did we see who?" Fi asked.

"There was a man. He was looking through Ann's window."

"A peeping Tom? That doesn't sound good," Charles exclaimed. "What did he look like?"

"He had dark skin and slick, black hair. He wore a light-colored suit."

"He was Indian?" Jeremy asked.

Victoria shook her head. "No, I don't think he

looked Indian. He just had a very nasty tan."

"I'm calling Ann!" Fi said, and walked to the kitchen to get the phone. There was an uneasy mood in the living room until she came back.

"Ann just checked in the garden. Victoria was right. Someone was there! There were fresh footprints in the snow just below the kitchen window. I made her promise that she'd call us if anything happens."

"Maybe it's safer if she stays here?" Victoria suggested.

"You are the one they want," Charles rationalized. "But you're right. I'll try to convince her to come stay with us for a few days. Maybe she can get some time off work." He looked at Fi.

Beate cleared her throat. "Can I have some of the powder too?"

"Of course you can. I prepared a bag for you. When you get home, you'll have to find a place where you can use the portal undisturbed. A place in your house and one in Victoria's. The first time you open the portal, your chosen sites will be connected to our kitchen."

"Does that mean we can only contact you here in your kitchen? And no one else but you?" Beate asked.

Charles shook his head. "In theory, there are no limits for linking the rings. However, it's complicated and quite dangerous if something goes wrong. So we've mixed your powder beforehand. This way, the powder and the rings are already locked in on each other."

"And what do I do now?" Victoria asked.

"First of all, I think you should talk to your mother and John about all this when you get home," Charles said.

"I don't think it's a good idea," Victoria said. "They won't understand. It will just make them really worried."

"Then perhaps it's better if I talk to them. We need their help to keep you safe," Fi said.

"I don't think they're ready to hear about the Carpathian brotherhood, and they're certainly not prepared to hear about a live, breathing thunderbird!"

"But she is your mother, and keeping the Carpathian threat from her doesn't seem right," said Fi.

"She'll probably think you've lost your marbles. That the grief from losing your son has made you both crazy. And then there will be no more trips to Canada!" said Beate.

"I think the girls are right," said Charles. "It's going to complicate everything if we tell them about this. Our only priority is to watch out for Victoria. It would be fatal if her mother decides we can't keep in touch."

Fi sighed.

"I'll call them tomorrow then and tell them it was nice having you.." She said.

She didn't look too happy about the decision.

"It's important that you carry on doing whatever you normally do, so that no one suspects anything. And it's important that you explore, and test, your new-found powers!" said Bill.

"I'll do that," Victoria promised.

"And we'll call you to hear about your progress," Mary Joan said.

Victoria swallowed hard. They all wanted to help her. In the old days medicine men in training had been lucky to have just one mentor. She had a whole team of people supporting her. Jeremy had called it her 'ring of protectors'. It was comforting; however, she was still scared of the Carpathians. Their web was intricate and extensive, and she didn't know what to expect next.

Could her guardians really protect her against them?

Would she and Beate be able to detect them if they were to contact her again? She felt uneasy.

Later that evening, Fi pulled Victoria aside.

"When you were there...in the cave, did you notice if anyone had been there recently? Any hints of what might have happened to him?"

Victoria put her hand on Fione's shoulder.

"No one had been to the cave for years, but still I sensed my dad's presence. I am sure he made it to the cave too. But I don't know what happened to him next. He must have left again on his own, because otherwise I would have found him there!"

"Deep in my heart I still feel that he is around," Fi sighed. "If only we knew what happened in that cave!"

Ullerslev, 24 December 2017

Dear Diary,

On our last night in Canada, Jeremy, Beate and I ended up in the hallway of my grandparents' house. The others had gone outside to warm up the car, and suddenly we were just standing there.

For a moment, no one said anything. It was a bit awkward.

Then Beate said she'd leave us two alone...!

What was she thinking?

I wanted to disappear.

However, there was nothing I could do but keep cool.

Beate gave Jeremy a big hug, asked him to add her on FB and Instagram, and then she left.

Then it was just Jeremy and me!

It's weird how he makes me unsure of myself. When he looks at me I lose the gift of speech and I just want to run away. Only running away is hard because I can't get my eyes of his smile either, and my feet won't move.

The silence was intense.

He then said he was going to miss me!

Yes, he did☺.

As usual, I didn't have a sweet or interesting answer to give him.

He stood there, with his fantastic smile, and said he would call me!

I remember promising him to be careful—and to call him if anything suspicious happened.

I wondered if perhaps he was going to kiss me, but then we were interrupted by his father who came to tell that they were all set to go☹.

Jeremy gave me a small, gift-wrapped box and sent me off with a "Merry Christmas, Thunderbird."

I know I told you that a relationship with Jeremy was doomed because he lives so far away. I'm taking that back. I don't care where he lives. He could live at the North Pole for all I care.

I just wish he was my boyfriend!

And why didn't I think of getting him a Christmas present?

I opened mine on the plane. It was a red plastic heart with 'missing you' written on it.

A bit cheesy, but when I showed it to Beate she just smiled secretively at me.

She spent hours with Jeremy on the boat, and she hasn't revealed a word of what they were talking about.

Some friend!

We arrived in Copenhagen at 3:30 in the morning. I hardly got any sleep during the flight because there was too much going on in my head. Instead, I must have read every Danish newspaper on the aircraft. Nothing much seemed to have happened while we were away. The most exciting news was probably an article about a party of rhinoceros thieves operating in Denmark.

Rhinoceros thieves!

According to the article, a gang of criminals had been stealing the rhinos' horns for export to the Far East. The sales value per kilo is higher than that of gold! The buyers turn the horns into a powder and use it for homeopathic medicine. Normally, I wouldn't have read this article but, because of my experiences in Canada, I now have to keep myself updated on anything out of the ordinary that happens.

Come on?

Ivory poachers in Denmark?

Anyway, my mom and John were happy to see me safely back home. Little do they know about what really happened over there....

They were a bit upset about the fact that I forgot to test my blood. Now we will have to get me a new appointment, and since the hospital is extremely busy, it might be months before they can fit me in. I'm not worried though, because now I know that there is nothing 'wrong' with me☺ and, despite their best intensions, those doctors won't be able to help.

In the meantime, I can't use the mixture.

What a bore!

But Fi and Charles were very strict. Even though I have the recipe for the mixture, we don't know when I'll be able to get hold of all the ingredients to make a new portion. So I have to save the little mixture I have for emergencies. We must also assume that the Carpathians are watching me, and there is no need for them to know that we now have the recipe too (and suddenly turning into a superwoman would be a certain giveaway).

It's hard!

I personally see it as the equivalent of telling Bruce Wayne that he can't visit the Bat Cave.

Or telling Popeye that he has to lay off spinach!

And then there's Jeremy!

The legends have always been part of his life and he quickly accepted that I was now a thunderbird.

Maybe a little too quickly if you ask me.

Before all this thunderbird business, he was just a cool guy who seemed to like me. Now he's one of my guardians. And I have a plastic heart telling me that maybe there is more to it—to us.

But how will I ever know whether he's interested in me as a girl or as the thunderbird?

Epilogue

ON A CITY STREET in Saint John, people had gathered in the greying evening light. Beneath a street lamp, a woman lay half-hidden in the snow.

When the police arrived, her body was already cold. They rolled her onto her back, revealing a face locked in an expression of terror.

A large pin with a matted mother of pearl pinhead was lodged in the victim's neck.

"That thing can't be the murder weapon!" said one of the police officers. He checked his notebook. "Witnesses saw two people fleeing the scene. One was a woman with long, black hair and the other a tanned man with slick, black hair in a light-colored coat."

"Whatever they were up to, they seem to have been interrupted," said the other officer, pointing to the handbag lying next to the woman.

Snow fell heavily while the two police officers sealed off the crime scene. When the ambulance arrived, a paramedic jumped from the vehicle before it came to a full stop. When he saw the woman's face, he made the sign of the holy cross.

"She looks as if she's seen the devil himself," he

exclaimed. Then he closed her eyes.

"Do we know who she is?"

"Yes, her name is Ann Hansson," said the officer who had looked through her handbag. "She's local, so it shouldn't be hard to locate, and inform, her next of kin."

A list of the most significant names

Passamaquoddy — one of the Indian tribes that make up the Abenaki people.

Victoria Hansson — 16 years old, thunderbird, and medicine woman, of the Passamaquoddy tribe.

Julie Hansson — Victoria's mother.

John — Victoria's stepfather.

Beate — 16 years old, Victoria's best friend.

Sarah — 16 years old, just moved in on Victoria's street. She and her large family originate from the southeastern parts of Europe.

Roberto — 18 years old, Sarah's older brother.

George Hansson — Victoria's father. Passamaquoddy Indian and believed dead. He disappeared in Canada when Victoria was eight years old.

Fione (Fi) — Victoria's grandmother. Passamaquoddy Indian, lives in New Brunswick, Canada.

Charles — Victoria's grandfather. Passamaquoddy Indian, lives in New Brunswick, Canada.

Ann Hansson — Victoria's Aunt. Passamaquoddy

Indian.

Bill Backsteps — Medicine man, one of the Passamaquoddy elders.

Peter Two Hawks — Friend of Victoria's late father, Fi and Charles. Penobscot Indian (a tribe that also belongs the Abenaki people).

Jeremy Two Hawks — 19 years old, Peter Two Hawks' older son.

Storm Two Hawks — 15 years old, Peter Two Hawks' younger son.

Mary Joan Steward — A historian with roots in the Penobscot tribe. She is very interested in Indian culture and history. She lives in New Brunswick, Canada.

Dr Dederich Schwartz — Medical specialist with a clinic based in Dresden, Germany. Member of the Carpathians' German chapter. (A chapter is a local division of the Carpathians' organization.)

The Wolf — One of the Carpathians' henchmen and a hired assassin. He is very tanned and always wears a light-colored suit and coat.

Diane Southby — Another Carpathian henchman operating in North America.

More books from
Harvard Square Editions:

People and Peppers, Kelvin Christopher James

Gates of Eden, Charles Degelman

Love's Affliction, Fidelis Mkparu

Transoceanic Lights, S. Li

Close, Erika Raskin

Anomie, Jeff Lockwood

Living Treasures, Yang Huang

Nature's Confession, J.L. Morin

Love and Famine, Han-ping Chin

Dark Lady of Hollywood, Diane Haithman

How Fast Can You Run, Harriet Levin Millan

Appointment with ISIL, Joe Giordano

Never Summer, Tim Blaine

Parallel, Sharon Erby

www.ingramcontent.com/pod-product-compliance
Lightning Source LLC
Chambersburg PA
CBHW061523020726
47502CB00006B/2197